PRAISE FOR
THE LAST FERRYMAN

"This is [Randle's] debut novel and a very good one."

—ALAN CARUBA, MEMBER OF NATIONAL BOOK CRITICS CIRCLE, *Bookviews*

"A beautifully detailed accounting of a lost way of life
. . . captivating . . . unforgettable . . . will touch the
hearts of readers."

—*Readers' Favorite*

"*The Last Ferryman* is a nice read; well written and well paced.
. . . This is a novel that has re-read value and one I'll be
keeping on my bookshelf."

—*San Francisco Book Review*

"A nice trip down memory lane. . . . I like it!"

—*Minnesota Public Radio News, The Daily Circuit Book Pick*

the L A S T
F E R R Y M A N

a novel

the L A S T
F E R R Y M A N

a novel

Gregory D. Randle

LANGDON STREET PRESS

MINNEAPOLIS, MN

Langdon Street Press
322 First Avenue N, 5th floor
Minneapolis, MN 55401
612.455.2293
www.langdonstreetpress.com

ISBN-13: 978-1-62652-493-4
LCCN: 2013953652

Distributed by Itasca Books

Cover Design by Kristeen Ott
Typeset by Jenni Wheeler

Printed in the United States of America

For Janelle

To every action, there is always an equal and opposite reaction.
—Isaac Newton, *The Principia*

But do you not mean that the river is everywhere at once, at its origins and at its mouth, at the waterfall, at the ferry, at the rapids, in the sea, in the mountains, everywhere at the same time, and for it only the present exists, no shadow of the past, no shadow of the future?
—Herman Hesse, *Siddhartha*

PROLOGUE

John Welch, despite his crusty, somewhat feral look, was a reader of newspapers. He subscribed to no less than five dailies: the *Terre Haute Tribune*, the *Sullivan Democrat*, the *Robinson Daily News*, the *Chicago Daily News*, and the best of the lot when it came to reporting on the latest bridge developments, the *Indianapolis News*. Welch also received the weekly *Millerville Gazette*, but he didn't consider it a true newspaper. He read it if for no other reason than to keep an eye on Dorothy Smith, who, along with her husband, Wilbur, was its publisher. She was capable of stirring up all manner of trouble.

From his reading, Welch knew when, in 1929, the citizens of Sullivan County, Indiana, formed a three-man bridge commission to fulfill a "long-felt need" for a connection from southern Indiana to communities in Illinois and, more important, Saint Louis, Missouri. The commission was granted the authority to engage engineers, offer bonds, and perform any other business requirements for such an undertaking.

The commission looked at Merom, Indiana, a few miles downriver from Millerville. The Indiana side looked good. There was already a road down to the river, following alongside the north face of the bluff. It would have to be improved, but the general outline was there. No surprise to Welch that Illinois wanted no part in the plan. It would require them to build up a road, at great expense, over a considerable stretch of low-lying bottomland. Merom as a bridge site was scuttled.

For reasons that were never entirely clear to Welch, talk of a bridge dropped out of the public discourse, completely disappearing off the pages of the newspapers. As people's attention turned to the Depression, the bridge seemed to be forgotten. Welch supposed the businessmen on the bridge commission had their own problems to attend to.

Unlike Welch, Buck Shyrock, the local ferryman, read no newspapers. He had a stubbornly held, abiding belief that any news worth knowing would be brought to him by one of his patrons. If he couldn't look the person in the eye, by his way of thinking, how could he make a judgment as to the reliability of the report? When Welch, crossing on the ferry one day, told Buck that Merom had been passed over as a site for a new bridge, Buck took it as fact. John Welch was someone he'd known from early on; he trusted Welch.

"Wouldn't that be somethin' if they chose Millerville?" Welch said carelessly, without thinking about the impact it might have on Shyrock.

"It won't happen. Not here."

"Why not?"

Digging at the hollow of his big ear, Buck said, "Not enough demand. I should be a judge o' that."

"But don't you reckon if they built a bridge, the need would arise? It'd spur growth, or so the thinking goes."

"It won't happen here," Buck said, his jaw set. "This is a ferry town, always has been, and it'll keep on bein' a ferry town."

Shyrock, Welch knew, simply couldn't imagine Millerville without a ferry. There had been a ferry crossing the river here since long before Shyrock and Welch's time. The first was a cable ferry, shunted across the river by the force of the current, operated by Shyrock's grandfather and then his father and which Buck himself had learned on, followed by the gasoline-propelled ferry Buck now piloted.

After a few moments, Buck shot a glance John Welch's way and grunted a kind of begrudging acknowledgment of the man's words. "Well, it'll be a long spell before a bridge comes here. After my time—that much is for certain."

The next nine years seemed to support Shyrock's way of thinking. Nothing more was heard about a bridge in Millerville, and the townspeople learned quickly not to mention anything to do with a bridge around Shyrock— not if they wanted a smooth landing on the opposite bank. Shyrock's mistake was to think that, like him, no one else could imagine the town without a ferry.

CHAPTER 1

THE RIVER SIGHS

An early mist shrouded the middle of the river—water and air became one. The old ferryman's lungs filled with the mist's fishy breath. He killed the motor and peered ahead, his head cocked, listening. After a time, he bent and coiled the rope around its pulley. Yanked it. The motor sputtered back to life.

Closer in to the bank, the mist thinned enough for the ferryman to spot him: a man—a stranger—standing in the willowy brush, five hundred feet or so north of the ferry run; a slouch hat pulled low against the weather; a brown mackintosh, collar up; a bundle of official-looking papers, the man studying them.

The hound at the ferryman's side lifted her wet nose, sniffed the air, and growled low in her throat.

The man on the bank noticed him looking and raised an arm in greeting. The sheaf of papers bucked and rolled in on itself. In awkward gloved hands, he came close to dropping it. The ferryman stared back at the man and then looked away without acknowledging him.

The hound whined and licked the back of the ferryman's rough hand, which hung big as a plate at his side. He ruffled her ear. "No good comin' from there," he grumbled.

Downstream, beyond the wide sandbar that pressed out into the bending river like a smooth flexed muscle, a fisherman's johnboat, its sound made silky by the mist, moaned through the present, already beginning its slow fade into the past.

≈ ≈ ≈

John Welch's battered pickup waited at the ferry landing. Welch slouched in the cab, whistling a breathy, unrecognizable tune through the few crooked teeth that remained in his head. He gazed intently at the spot where the ferryboat would materialize out of the mist—first its apron, angled upward to match the exact slope of the riverbank, then its forward deck and weathered board railings, and finally, Buck Shyrock standing erect and solid as a tree trunk in the steer boat. Every fiber of the ferry operator's soul would be focused on the single task of landing the ferry straight and smooth against the Indiana riverbank, despite the hard nose of the current pushing at its side. Welch, with his window cracked open, could hear the motor out in the middle of the river, fighting the current, wheezing in the soupy air like a tired lung.

And then the motor stopped. Welch shook his head, muttered "Soppy ol' fugger" against a rising swell of tobacco juice, and then reached down to the floorboard and retrieved an old rusty coffee tin. He spat and set it down again.

A few minutes later, the motor stammered back to life. Not long after, the boat emerged out of the mist, exactly as Welch had pictured it, the ferry and its pilot as timeless as the river itself. As the ferry apron eased onto the sand, Welch began lowering his window. The worn crank mechanism on the old truck moved in fits and jerks, the window glass screeching in its frame. Once it opened enough for his narrow, wizened face to poke through, Welch bellowed, "Shyrock! There y'are!"

"What'd ya expect?" Shyrock shouted back.

"Expected ya sooner is what I expected. Your motor quit. Run into some trouble out there?"

As was often the case, the ferry operator pretended not to hear him. Leaving the idling motor to hold the deck in place against the landing, Shyrock grabbed hold of an upright and squeezed his thick frame through a space in the railing. In knee-high black gumboots, he tramped the length of the deck and unhitched one end of the log chain barrier draped across the end of the ferry. Welch sat gunning his engine, but the pilot refused to be rushed. By the time Shyrock reached the other end of the ferry and turned to direct him onto the deck, Welch had lurched his truck over the apron and onto the runner planks.

"I never knew it to take you so dad-blamed long, Shyrock," Welch complained as he gimped to the rail and opened his mouth enough to let the chaw of tobacco drop into the river.

Shyrock's hound jumped onto the deck from the steer boat. She sauntered up to Welch and sniffed his pant leg. Welch patted her on the head. Her curiosity satisfied, she returned to the corner of the ferry nearest the steer boat and collapsed in a jumble of bones and long, heaving sighs.

"I gathered it was you, so I took m'time," Buck said. He dropped a four-by-four beam behind the rear wheel of the truck and re-slung the barrier chain. "And jist ta remind ya, reg'lations say I'm ta die-rect you onta the boat."

Welch leaned against the fender of his truck and pulled a King Edward from his barn coat. He lifted his boot, scratched a match against its heel, and pulled at the cigar until it was lit. With a cool flick of his wrist, he tossed the match into the river. He smacked his lips, feigning supreme satisfaction with his cigar and himself.

With a lurching step, Buck dropped down into the steer boat.

"You're gettin' too old for this, Shyrock."

"You worry 'bout your own self, Welch."

"I ain't worried. I just don't want you breakin' a limb so I can't be delivered across the river when I feel the need."

"Don't push your luck, Welch. More'n one's offered ta pay me a healthy sum if I'd drop ya in Indiana and leave ya there."

Besides his rented-out farmland in Illinois and a few head of cattle he fattened in a pasture across the road from his house, Welch owned an eighty-acre piece over in the Indiana flood plain. Because of its seasonal deposit of flood-borne silt, it was some of the richest soil in the river valley. Problem was, come planting time, it was more often than not underwater. Teasingly, Shyrock called it the mudflats. Welch said it paid for itself and refused to get riled.

Shyrock swung the rear of the steer boat around so it faced the heart of the channel. He dropped the motor into gear with a hard *ka-chunk* that jarred the entire ferry and eased the throttle forward. "Feller on the bank over yonder," he said, jerking his head to indicate the spot.

Welch turned to look. He knew in an instant what it meant.

Through the thinning mist, the stranger back on the riverbank, seeing Welch watching him, raised a hand in greeting. Welch touched the brim of his hat and nodded. "There it is then," Welch said.

He looked at Shyrock, whose only response was to narrow his eyes and to look even more intently at the river ahead, just off the ferry's prow. *No use saying anything more,* Welch thought. Shyrock would need time to chew on this new turn of events.

In the time it took Buck to land the ferry and moor it to the cement landing that cut steeply down from the high Illinois bank, the mist had lifted to become a part of the gray smudgy sky, leaving the river to its own devices.

Welch looked back across the channel. The man trudged up the riverbank, papers tucked under his arm, pushing the young willows aside as he went. Welch tossed his partially smoked cigar into the river and climbed into his truck, ready for the return to solid ground. He cleared his throat. "We'll go fishin'," he said to Shyrock through the open truck window, because he had to say something. Welch would swear, on a stack of Bibles even, that just then he heard the river sigh.

LOG ENTRY: 10 January, 1939. I, Floyd Bailey, project engineer for the state of Indiana, hereby begin my personal record of the bridge construction about to commence on the Wabash River at Millerville, Illinois.

Armed with a roll of bridge plans, I reported to the bridge site on a day that started out foggy and turned chillier as the day progressed. It was easy to locate the bridge site as shown on the plans, but it required an elastic imagination to visualize the lines of the graceful bridge that is to rise where now there are only weeds and underbrush and a sparse line of trees.

I made a general inspection of the site. The main river channel is approximately 400 feet wide at this point. The main current and deepest part of the channel is near the west bank, which is higher than normal flood elevation. East of the channel is a low bank, rising about 10 feet above low water elevation, extending back about 500 feet to the toe of a high levee, which was built to keep floodwater from covering about 25 square miles of low-lying farmland.

The bridge designed for this crossing is a new type of structure. It is a self-anchoring suspension bridge, consisting of a 350-foot main span and two 150-foot anchor spans. The east approach to the suspension spans consists of seven continuous steel-girder viaduct spans of 50 feet each.

The viaduct spans are to be built on a level grade from the east abutment, which is at the levee, to the east anchor open pier, which is on the low east bank about 120 feet from the low water channel. From this point, the east anchor span is to rise on a plus 6 percent grade to the main span, which is to be built to a parabolic curve between the plus 6 percent grade of the east anchor span and the minus 6 percent grade on the west anchor span.

The bridge floor is 20 feet wide between curbs, with a narrow sidewalk on each side. This width of roadway is approved for class A bridges.

The suspension span of this bridge has no concrete anchorages but was designed so the horizontal component of the cable tension is taken by axial compression in the stiffening girders. Besides having this unique characteristic of being self-anchoring, this structure has several other features that make it of unusual interest to an engineer like me. A few of these are the use of 94-foot steel H-beam piles; the use of a thin, concrete-filled I-beam floor; and the use of a single expansion joint for the 1,000 feet of steel superstructure.

CHAPTER 2

THE IVY LEAF

The girls came screaming to him out of the kitchen. August gathered them up and held them to his chest, giving each of them a peck on the cheek.

"You're scwatchy, Daddy" the youngest, Vivian, said, rubbing his stubbled chin with the back of her dimpled little hand.

Nine-year-old Holly sniffed at his neck. "You smell like dust," she said. There was no judgment in her voice, no complaint.

"I wike the way Daddy smells."

"I didn't say I didn't like it," Holly said, bristling.

August sniffed each of his daughters' hair. "I like the way you two smell. Like flowers," he said. "Like Daddy's very own flower garden."

"I'm not a fwowa, I'm not a gawden eitha," Vivian said, squirming to be let down. She slipped through August's arm like sand sifting out the bottom of a sack. "I'm a guh-wol."

August set her down but held on to Holly. Vivian ran back into the kitchen. "Daddy's home, Mommy," she announced.

"You can call me your flower garden, Daddy," Holly said, her blue-gray eyes—his father's eyes—burrowing their light into him. "I don't mind."

"Thank you, precious girl," August said and kissed her on her dark curls. "Let's see about your mother."

"We've got supper," Holly said, holding his hand, walking with him into the kitchen.

The kitchen was the largest room of the house, open and cheerful, where August and Belle and their girls spent most of their time together as a family. The table was set with flower-painted plates and silverware perfectly straight. Belle was teaching the girls how to do things right.

August felt a rush of gratitude to have all that he had.

≈ ≈ ≈

After supper, when the girls had been scrubbed, cuddled, and kissed and then put to bed, Belle and August sat in the living room, enjoying the quiet ending of their day.

"I don't reckon you've heard the news," August said.

"News? In Millerville! Do tell."

August smiled at her pertness. "A fella showed up, looking around over across the river. Papers in his hand."

"Did you see him?" Belle stood up. Barefoot, she crossed the room and pulled a wilted leaf from an ivy plant. August watched her—her straight, taut shoulders, her slenderness, her easy way of moving through the world. How had he gotten hold of her, this rare, glistening gem of a woman? A ferryman's son, with the muddy smell of the river still clinging to him at the time, no less.

"Did I see him? No. But he was all the talk."

Belle returned to her chair, close by August, and tucked one leg under her. August sipped on his evening mug of tea.

"You know what this means," August said.

"Yes. It's hard to imagine, isn't it?" She turned the ivy leaf in her hand, rubbing its dry, curled edges between her slender finger and thumb.

August nodded, trying to picture such a thing. Where now there was only air and sky and water, an actual bridge, a mass of steel and poured concrete, would cross the river, dropping down next to the hardware store, intersecting with Main Street.

"What did he look like? Anyone say?"

"No, they couldn't see that much. Tall."

"You know what else this means then," Belle said.

"Yeah, of course I know what else it means." An edge came into his voice, a rare thing when they talked.

Belle laid her hand on top of August's rough hand. "You have to talk to him."

"You think so."

"I hate to tell you, darling, but you're it—his only son, his only child." She grasped his hand in hers. "There's no one else."

August knew she was right. But the thought of talking with his dad about this, of all things. "Oh, Christ. I'll do it tomorrow," he said. "First thing."

CHAPTER 3

THE ENGINEER

John Welch recognized him immediately as the man he and Shyrock had spotted yesterday on the riverbank. He was leaning over his breakfast at the counter of Thompson's Drugstore, forking eggs into his mouth like a hungry foot soldier. Welch settled onto a stool one down from him and, catching his eye, nodded his head in greeting. The man, thirtyish, still caught in that fine balance between youthful energetic good looks and the weight and responsibilities of early middle age, smiled at him and began mopping up egg yolk with his toast.

"By the way you make full use of your toast," Welch said by way of introduction, "I reckon you're from somewhere here in the valley."

"You have a keen eye," the man said. He wiped his hand on a napkin and reached across the empty bar stool between them. "Floyd. Floyd Bailey. Born and raised just over in Sullivan."

"John Welch. Been here in Millerville my whole life. Except for a stint in the navy." In shaking Bailey's hand, Welch noticed it didn't carry the hard, leathery roughness that it would have if he made his living by the bent of his back. Instead, his hands were fine and lean-fingered. *Good hands for playing piano*, Welch mused. Bailey carried an intelligent look—an educated man, no doubt. The fact that he hadn't shaved this morning roughened his appearance somewhat.

"A navy man. You've been in a war."

"Is it obvious?"

"Something about a war veteran. You don't look so naïve as the rest of us. You've seen how bad it can get."

"With this Depression, plenty have had a taste, I'm afraid," Welch said.

"It's not the same, I don't think," Floyd insisted. He lifted his mug and slurped coffee. "What war were you in?"

"Spanish-American. Served under Commodore Schley on the USS *Brooklyn*. A gunner at the Battle of Santiago de Cuba."

"Very impressive," Floyd said, his voice sincere. "You kicked their rears in that one."

"We suffered our losses."

"Hmm," Floyd said. "I bet you have stories to tell. I wouldn't mind hearing them sometime." He pushed his plate away and sighed. "I think I'll be stopping here again."

"I believe you're with the bridge," Welch said, prying a bit.

Floyd nodded. "Project engineer, state of Indiana."

"Impressive," Welch said, returning the compliment.

"Not as impressive as a naval victory. And only if you consider looking over the shoulder of the company engineer impressive."

"Besides the navy, I've been a dirt farmer my whole life." Welch gave him a flat look. "It don't take much."

Floyd laughed. "My grandpa was a farmer. He didn't impress easily at all. Said college would ruin me. It's been fifteen years, and I still haven't decided if he was right or not."

Sal Thompson set a steaming mug of coffee in front of Welch. "Good morning, Sir John," she said. Sal was a friendly, comely woman, well into her middle years. She was dressed in her usual: a pressed, well-starched, white waitress dress. With her husband permanently disabled by a coal mining accident, she took her business seriously and dressed accordingly. "Same old same old?"

"Wouldn't want to confuse you, my dear."

"Go ahead; confuse me," she said. "Good exercise for my brain."

"Too busy confusin' myself," Welch answered, tipping cream into his cup.

Sal offered Floyd more coffee. He waved her off. "Too much and I'll hurt myself. Jitters, you know."

"Sorry, but I couldn't help eavesdropping," she said, leaning forward on the counter between the two men. "So you're the bridge guy I heard about."

"Guilty as accused."

"How long is it gonna take to build, ya think?"

"Oh, if everything goes right, if the river cooperates and all, it should take about a year, maybe less, from start to finish."

Welch looked around the drugstore. Everyone in the place, even those sitting back along the side wall in the dim row of booths, was watching and listening.

"The surveyors will be showing up today," Floyd said. "That's the start."

Sal looked at Welch with a dreamy look. "A bridge, John; imagine that," she said.

"Yep, hard to believe," Welch said. "So, Floyd," he asked after Sal had left them, "where did you get your engineering degree?"

"Rose Tech," Floyd answered. He pulled out his wallet and fished around for money.

"Rose Polytechnic Institute, in Terre Haute?" Welch whistled through his teeth. "Now I *am* impressed. Only the best and brightest pass through those hallowed doors. Local boy makes good."

Floyd shrugged off the compliment. *Intelligent but humble,* Welch thought. *Good traits in a man.* He liked this Floyd Bailey already.

Floyd stood up, looked at his ticket, dropped money on the counter, and then stuck out his hand to Welch. "John, I hope to continue our conversation another day. Seriously, I wouldn't mind hearing some war stories—that is, if you feel so inclined. This is where you'll find me just about every morning until the bridge is built." He glanced around the drugstore with a conspiratorial look and leaned toward Welch. "Don't repeat that I said this, but the great state of Indiana, my noble employer, likes to think this will be their bridge. We know better."

With a wave of his hand that seemed to include everyone, he hurried out the door, an air of seriousness already descending upon him.

Watching him go, Welch realized that he was looking forward to his next breakfast with the young engineer, when he would query him about the particulars of bridge building.

With the thought came a pang of guilt. By taking such an unbridled interest in the bridge, was he somehow being disloyal to Shyrock? Millerville couldn't remain in the past, Welch knew. But as friends go, Buck Shyrock was his closest. A slippery slope—very slippery indeed.

Sal slid his breakfast in front of him. "That bridge is really gonna change this town," she said excitedly.

"I hope not too much," Welch said. "We might not be able to recognize it."

Refilling his coffee, Sal looked at him quizzically and then moved away to wait on customers who had just sat down.

CHAPTER 4

DUTY COMES FIRST

They sat at the kitchen table, not quite facing one another, the vestige of an old antagonism between them that ran deep, that neither fully understood and thus couldn't fix. Already back from bringing a farmer and his wagonload of corn across the river, August's father had taken off his rubber boots, and they stood erect, side by side, almost regal, like two old loyal servants next to his chair. The hound he had taken in as a stray lay in a thin strip of pale sunshine marking the floor. Dust motes floated in the air above her like loose threads snipped and released from a dream. The ray of light revealed how badly the floor needed cleaning. *The whole house could use a cleaning,* August thought, looking around the dusty kitchen and into the parlor.

August didn't know where to start. *Just dive in, man.* "I reckon you saw him yesterday. Over on the Indiana side."

"I reckon I did."

August waited for his father to say more, but he continued to look down at his coffee cup, turning it on its saucer, waiting for the liquid to cool, his face blank, unreadable.

Stubborn old bastard.

After a time, his father poured coffee, steaming, into the saucer. He blew on it and poured it back into the cup.

The china, holdovers from August's mother's time, looked almost like a child's tea set in his massive hands. August remembered, as a teenager, slipping his hand into one of his father's work gloves—gloves he'd found stuffed in a cupboard because his father never wore them. Dejected, he'd thought to himself, *My hands will never be this big, not in a million years.*

His father sipped, found the coffee too hot still, and set the cup down again. "You come over here just to look at me, son? What's on your mind? Spill it."

"Dad, you can quit. Retire. You've earned it, you know." Hearing himself say it, it sounded ridiculous, somehow, leaving his mouth. The old man hardly ever left the river's edge, except when he leaned his "Back Directly" sign—scratched on a scrap of two-by-sixteen plank—at the end of the ferry rail and hurried up to Main Street to the post office, to Solner's Grocery, or to McNutt's Hardware for some repair part or other needed on the ferry.

"So now you're plannin' my life for me? Is that it?"

August could just walk out right now. He thought of Belle. "Dad, don't you ever want more out of life? You never go anywhere. You could come and go as you please. How do you keep from going loony, anyway?" As soon as he'd said these last words, he knew he'd overstepped a boundary. He'd not just asked a question and offered a suggestion, but he'd laid down a judgment.

Buck rose from the table and plodded in stocking feet to the window overlooking the river, a habit he'd had for as long as August could remember. When August was a child, his mother had scolded Buck for it, always getting up from the table to peer out the window. "Stephen, they'll let you know if they're there," she would chide. *Duty comes first*. That's what he was thinking then and what he still thought.

Buck turned and faced August, his wide shoulders nearly blocking the light from the window. "Loony, ya say?"

"Dad, that's not what I said. I didn't say you're loony."

"Well, if I had ta sit on my backside all day, lookin' out a truck window, I *would* go loony."

Here we go, August thought. He took a breath and then released it. "I don't sit on my backside all day."

Yes, here it was, the essence of their ongoing skirmish, father and son. August had chosen not to follow the family tradition. Begrudgingly, he had learned the ferrying trade from his father, but as soon as he finished school, he followed through on what he'd been planning but had kept to himself for some time: he moved out of the house and got a job working on the township road crew. His father had never quite forgiven him for it.

The old man turned away from him and looked out the window again.

"All right, Dad. Suit yourself." He had tried. Belle couldn't say he hadn't. "Well, I'm off. Gotta go sit in my truck." August attempted a laugh, but it fell flat, coming out surly. He picked up his coffee cup and saucer to carry them to the counter by the wash pan.

"Leave it," Buck said.

August had never quite understood why, even as an adult, something in him rebelled against following any command given by his father—he only knew it was somehow related to the ferry. Today, though, he would cut the old man some slack. That much he could do. He set the cup and saucer back on the table.

"Give them girls a kiss for me," Buck said, his voice softening. "And Belle, too."

"I can do that." *Stubborn old bastard. Soft on the girls and Belle— and, oh yes, the dog. Spoils it something terrible; wouldn't be surprised if he lets it sleep in his bed—and hard as nails on anything else, including me.*

"*Think you're too good for it,*" he'd said the day August told him he was leaving home. "*Too good for it; too good for your mother and me.*"

His mother hadn't blamed him, though—a young man harnessed to a ferry for the rest of his days when he didn't want to be. It was in her eyes: sad for her husband's loss of him but glad for her only son.

Walking out to his truck, August thought how he himself had avoided, for his father's sake, the word *bridge.* Like it was poison, as though an earth swell would burst up from under the floorboards if it were spoken aloud. Probably only one person in the whole valley felt that way, and it had to be his old man.

CHAPTER 5

A PANG THROUGH HIS HEART

Buck sat in his kitchen, his boots beside him, his hound sprawled at his feet, trying not to think of the changes coming his way. He had stoked up the fire in the wood stove and now moved his chair closer, waiting for it to take the chill off the house.

The house, provided to Shyrock as partial compensation for his official duties as ferry operator, lacked any of the modern conveniences. He still used a hand pump in the kitchen. He heated his water and cooked his meals over a mammoth, sooty, wood cookstove. An unpainted privy stood out back of the house next to Water Street, a narrow, curving lane that backed Main Street. Some joker with too much time on his hands had painted in dripping white letters on the outhouse's weathered back, *"Fares Took Here."*

Without feeling the need to explain, Buck had refused offers by Faber McNutt, the actual ferry owner, to modernize the "ferry house," as the locals called Buck's home.

Now, sitting in the dim, antiquated kitchen, Buck felt as if the house's emptiness—its hollows, its echoes, its musty drafts, its long shadows—since his Ida had passed had crept into a cavity in his chest, next to his heart, and taken up residence there.

Ida and Buck were married forty years. *Perfect* was the word he thought of to describe their union, although he knew it hadn't all been perfect. But in the early days, it had been just that. He had courted Ida, walking to her family's farm on Sundays, wearing a suit and a newer version of the newsboy cap he still wore. He looked the dandy, even though he'd had to scrub himself with a brush to get the river smell off of him. He was nineteen years old.

They fell in love quickly. He wanted to touch her in the worst way, and she him. It was like a fever. Even when her family was around—in the house, outside in the yard—his hands nearly screamed in their desire to reach out and caress Ida. When they were finally allowed to be alone, walking down the dirt lane behind the farm, Ida whispered to him her identical desire: her hands craved the feel of him. At the end of the lane, where the wheel tracks petered out in the loose dust, giving way to a single walking path that wound through low brush and then to woods, they were free to let their hands do as they wished.

They were married six months before baby Elizabeth was born. The day she arrived, Buck's father died, never having fully recovered from the croupous pneumonia he had contracted a few years earlier.

And then, only three days later, their Elizabeth. Dark days. Heavy, dark days. All these years later, he could still barely stand to think about it. Most of the time, he was able to hide it away, to turn his mind away from it.

They moved into the house above the ferry landing, and Buck took over as ferryman. They lived there with his mother, who was quiet as dust after the death of his father. Ida nursed her until finally, she too passed on.

August was born a year almost to the day after losing Elizabeth. Ida barely let him out of her sight in the first years of his life, as if death, forever preying on babies and defenseless children, was her personal enemy. He was not allowed to stay overnight at any of his schoolmates' houses; Ida required instead that the other children come to the ferry house. Since it was such a one-way exchange, the overnights with each friend gradually dwindled away.

When August was down at the river with him, Buck could feel Ida watching from the window, trying to keep the child in her sight by leaning when he disappeared behind the bank. Buck believed that August picked up on his mother's ambivalence toward his being at the river. This, of course, became a point of friction between the two parents, and Buck eventually blamed Ida when his son grew to despise the life of a ferryman.

They persevered, however, and the child was raised without serious sickness or poor health. Ida didn't relax until August turned fifteen. By then, he was a husky, vibrant young man, and she finally believed he would make it into adulthood.

The rest of their years together in the ferry house were good years. She continued in her habit of calling Buck "Daddy," even after August had moved out, and except during the occasional spat that lasted at most a day or two, she said it with real affection in her voice.

Four years ago, Ida died of her very first sugar diabetes attack. Buck, August, and Belle had tried to get her to the doctor at the first sign of problems—blurred vision, excessive thirst, an insatiable appetite for sugar—but she had flatly and stubbornly refused. Finally, when her blurred vision advanced to seeing double and she could no longer stand on her own, they walked her to the car. But it was too late.

She lapsed into a coma shortly after arriving at the hospital and never regained consciousness. None of them had had the slightest idea that it was diabetes they were dealing with.

The dog reached with her hairy paw and laid it softly atop Buck's gnarly foot, as if she was trying, gently, to divert his attention away from such a burdensome train of thought. Buck bent forward in his chair, took the hound's paw in his hand, and swung it gently from side to side. All he had now by way of companionship was this ol' hound. A good companion she was, though.

She had come to him six months after Ida passed. As Buck was approaching the Indiana landing to pick up a waiting car and its passengers, the dog had raised her snout to the sky and howled sorrowfully. It was a bluetick, a coon hunter if trained early enough. Buck could see straight away the dog's ribs pressing out against her mottled hide. She had worms, that much was clear. Plus, once he'd landed the ferry and got a closer look, he could see the bare, mangy patch on her left hind leg.

The hound sat back on her haunches and scratched at an ear. After the car pulled onto the ferry deck, she followed, prancing up to Buck as if this was exactly what she had been waiting to do.

"Your dog?" he asked the driver of the car, even though he knew better. The dog had been cared for poorly, if at all, and most likely was dumped somewhere on one of the deserted roads that wound through the river bottoms and eventually petered out in some overgrown weed patch like a bad idea.

"Nope," the man said. "She was here when we showed up. A stray, looks like. Never seen a motlier-lookin' creature."

When the dog sat down in front of him, looking frankly into his face as if to say, *What now?*, Buck moved a back leg aside with his boot and peeked past her pink hairless stomach to confirm what he'd guessed: the hound was indeed a bitch.

"I'll tell ya this much," he said, meeting the dog's gaze. "You go with me over ta my place, and I'll feed you some grub 'til your owner shows up and takes you back home." But he knew there was no owner coming to claim this half-starved, mangy, flea-bitten animal. He wasn't ready to admit it to himself, but he had already decided to keep her.

As soon as Buck dropped into the steer boat and started across the river, the hound lay on her belly on the ferry deck next to him. Her drooping black ears flapped in the wind.

"What's your name, ol' girl?" He reached over and scratched her on top of the head. "Not gonna tell me, huh? Gonna make me guess." He thought for a moment. "Blue," he said.

He watched for a sign of recognition from the dog. She continued to look straight ahead. She yawned and then snapped at a fly buzzing around her head. She caught it on her long, pink-and-gray tongue and swallowed it lavishly.

"Not Blue. Too easy."

Buck flipped up one of her ears and peered inside. A flea jumped out onto his hand and leaped away. He stuck his thick index finger roughly into the hound's ear and then sniffed his finger. No infection. He did the same with the other ear. She shook her head, her ears slapping mightily at the sides of her bony skull. Buck scratched the dog on the head again. He had always thought if he were ever to get a dog, it would be a bluetick.

He leaned toward the hound and said quietly, "Just between you and me, that feller don't know a good dog when he sees one."

Once home, he tried several more names, watching for her ears to pick up. When they didn't, he gave up. Because of the way she looked out upon the world, as if she knew precisely what it was about and didn't find it the least bit interesting, he landed on Rebel. "If you end up stayin', your name's gonna be Rebel. If you don't like it, you can leave."

But she didn't leave. From then on, she never left his side. He fed her beef bones, with sinewy strings of fresh red meat clinging to them, and thick slabs of bacon fat, for which he paid a half-cent a pound at Solner's Grocery, where he did his regular trading. And from a man he knew who worked in the oil fields over in the western part of the county, he picked up a jar of crude oil, which he rubbed on the dog's mange. In a few days, the raw, unsightly spot on her leg was gone, and the fur had begun growing back in, full as ever. For worms, he forced Days O' Work chewing tobacco down her gullet. Fleas? Mashed garlic cloves rubbed vigorously into her coat sent the little vermin packing within two shakes of her skinny tail. After the pungent flea treatment, Buck tried making her sleep out on the porch, but she created such a ruckus, howling and moaning, he finally relented and brought her, stinking to high heaven, back in the house to sleep by his bed. He slept with his arm over his face for two nights running.

For everyone except Buck, she peered out of her blocky head with the same droll, bored look. For him, though, from the first time she stepped foot on the ferry, her amber-colored eyes gazed upon him, as pure as pure can be, with something akin to love.

So the die was cast; she was his dog. Right away, Rebel began riding in the steer boat with Buck like it was her rightful spot, her long ears flapping and billowing in the wind like sails. Now and again, for no apparent reason, she would place her paws up on the channel side of the steer boat and bay out over the river, as if boasting to the world about her special, privileged rank on the Millerville ferryboat.

Once the fire had warmed the kitchen, Buck stood up, feeling the stiffness in his muscles and joints. John Welch was right—he was getting old—but he disagreed with Welch that he was too old to pilot the ferry. And August—*retirement!* A pang passed through his heart.

More men had shown up on the riverbank over in Indiana. That fella from the first day was with them. They carted around and set up surveying equipment.

A bridge. He couldn't make his thinking go any farther than that. *A bridge.* He tried saying it. "A bridge," he said to Rebel. He felt the words take shape in his mouth. Saying it was easy enough. Only two words.

Rebel raised her head off the floor and looked at him attentively. When he said nothing more, she laid her head back down and sighed, slowly and with meaning. Or so it seemed to Buck.

"Ol' girl, how'd you get stuck to me?" Buck said and then traipsed to the icebox to get her some supper.

CHAPTER 6

WHEN ALL IS SAID AND DONE

Virgil White talked with a hand-rolled cigarette dangling from his lip. "When my time comes," he said, "and it's comin' soon, hallelujah and Yankee Doodle Dandy, I will've earned myself the old-age pension." He removed his hat all of a sudden and held it over his bony chest. "Thankee, Mr. Roozavelt," he said, "thankee much," and dropped his hat back on his head. "He might be a rich bugger hisself, but he's a real workin' man's president when it comes right down to it. He's got my vote."

Despite his vigorous way of talking, Virgil looked unwell. Baked by years of hard sun, deep lines crisscrossed Virgil's face. Beneath the brown crust of his skin resided a gray, clammy pall. Liver spots dotted the sides of his crinkled forehead and neck and, growing smaller as they went, sprinkled down inside the collar of his loose-fitting shirt. Watching him bend to his work, August thought of inquiring after his health. As the township road commissioner, he was Virgil's boss, and he could (and probably should) ask, but he didn't believe it was his place to pry. The old-timer did his work.

August and Virgil were clearing saplings from around a culvert that ran under the township road. Virgil sliced through them with an axe, stopping to talk now and then, catching his breath, or rolling a cigarette. August muscled the fledgling stumps out of the stiff, hoary ground with a shovel, so come spring, they wouldn't grow back—their roots and swelling trunks eventually could stave in the culvert and shove it upwards from its station, ruining the road above.

"We shoulda did this earlier in the season," Virgil said, watching the point of August's shovel battling with the semi-frozen ground.

"We shoulda done a lot of things earlier," August answered. "Not enough hands, not enough time, and never enough of a lotta things." Because of the hard financial times, August had had to let a man go. That left the work to just him and Virgil, when three men hadn't been enough.

Virgil yanked at a cut sapling still hanging on by a strip of bark. It snapped free, nearly upending him. He tossed it off to the side. "I've worked hard my whole life," he said, steering their conversation back to his favorite topic: quitting work, having earned a rest. "And so has your dad. When that new bridge is finally built, he can hang up his hat." Virgil straightened his bent back and stretched. He looked August full in the face, something he rarely did. August could see him summoning up a passion that dwelt hidden in his grizzled soul, carried by one old laborer for another. "With honor," he pronounced, his voice thick with the moment, "hang it up with honor." He spoke as if August's father stood before him, and he was about to bestow upon him some working man's brand of a lifetime-achievement award. *An engraved, gold-plated shovel. Or maybe a bronzed coil of rope, mounted on polished wood. That would be good*, August thought, despite himself, caught up in the moment.

"That's what I tried to tell him," August said. "He won't talk about it. He's gotta be the most stubborn man ever lived."

"He comes by it honestly, m'boy. Your granddaddy was an ornery cuss. Maybe the river makes 'em that way; I don't know. Not an easy life, I reckon." Virgil yanked the half-burnt cigarette out of his mouth. He flicked with his tongue at a tiny piece of tobacco stuck to his lower lip and then spat. "And your daddy came to it early. After old Earl died."

Virgil turned to his work. His eyes flicked sideways at August as he sized up his next words and whether he should utter them at all. He didn't like bringing up the dead. No good could come of it. He chopped once at a sapling, stayed bent over, and said it anyway. "And losin' your baby sister the way they did."

"He never talks about that either," August said. *"The first baby,"* his mother always called her. Elizabeth. Perfectly healthy. Three days old. A commotion in the hospital corridor. Running, a lot of running. Toward the nursery, where the babies were kept separate from the mothers. His mother said she knew. And she did know.

"I gotta admit, Virgil, I'm worried about him." August bent toward a small stump and started hacking at its roots with the working end of his shovel. "He's not even close to being ready to quit."

"That don't matter much when all is said and done. Maybe he'll warm to the idea." Virgil shrugged his shoulders, ready to be done with the topic, a gesture that August didn't find consoling.

August pictured his old man standing in front of the window this morning, looking down at the river, waiting for a chance to escape the confines of the house, to get away from him and his talk. *Talk never got nobody nowhere. Only words.* His dad in a nutshell.

"My wife thinks it's my job to help him with that, to help him warm to the idea," August persisted. "I'm not so sure 'bout that."

"Good luck, m'boy," Virgil said. "Like I said, he sure do deserve it." Virgil chopped again at the sapling. It trembled and shook, as if feeling real pain, and then unceremoniously fell to the ground, its short life over.

CHAPTER 7

SILK ON SANDSTONE

"What did you say to him?"

August didn't like the way Belle said it, like she was accusing him of something.

"I said he can retire. That he's earned it."

"What did he say?"

"He said I'm tryin' to plan his life for him. Told me to mind my own business."

"He did not! Dad wouldn't—"

"Belle," he said, cutting her off. August was starting to get irritated with her now. He didn't like the line of questioning, the "your dad can do no wrong" tone of her voice. "Belle, he's stubborn. He's hard-headed. No one can tell him anything. When I tried, he same as called me a loony."

"A loony," Belle said. "Don't be ridiculous."

"Now I'm bein' ridiculous. First, I'm lying, and now I'm bein' ridiculous." August jerked up from his chair, spilling tea onto his pant leg. "Why don't *you* go next time!"

Belle followed him into the kitchen. "Auggie, I'm sorry. I didn't mean it that way." She took the mug from his hand and set it by the sink. She guided him gently to the table, and they both sat down, him at the end, her next to him.

Belle laid both her hands on top of August's, folded in front of him on the table. August breathed in and then released it, settling himself down.

"Look, we have to stick together on this," she said. "Dad can make it through this; I know he can. But he's gonna need our help."

"I don't know if I can help him. He doesn't want my help." August looked at her hands, warm and soft, on his own rough mitts, like silk on sandstone.

"He needs help. He wants help. He just doesn't know it yet."

"And how does he come to know it, Florence Nightingale?"

She slapped the top of his hand and laughed. "He will, and when he does, we need to be ready."

They went to bed after that. First, a wisp of cotton slid to the floor; then she lay down, smelling of lilac, cupped in against him, naked, the whole length of her warm and electric against his skin. As he lay there, cherishing the live, buzzing feel of her flesh on his, the old man, alone in the empty house, flashed unbidden through August's mind. Had his dad ever felt this surge of love and bold passion for August's mother? Obviously, he had. August's own existence was at least some testament to that. *Well, we have something in common at least.* August turned in bed and ran his middle finger and thumb down each side of his wife's perfect spine, its hard spindles cushioned by the toned muscles of her back, so soft yet so firm. He reached her tailbone. She breathed into his ear and flicked her tongue. *All so perfect,* he thought, his hand still going.

LOG ENTRY: 13 January, 1939. In assisting with the surveying, I checked the elevations that the designing engineers used and found they had made an error of about 3 feet in using a government benchmark. Consequently, elevations at the bridge were revised, and it was found the main span could be lowered and still have the required clearance above low-water elevation. The grade of the anchor spans could be reduced from a 6 percent grade to a 5 percent grade, thus improving the appearance of the bridge and making it safer to the driving public by increasing sight distance.

CHAPTER 8

THE SEER

No sooner had Holly arrived home from school than her mother sent her on an errand. Belle stood over a clean pile of laundry she'd dumped on the kitchen table. Her hands moved quickly and efficiently, folding and tucking, her lines straight and crisp. The kitchen was enveloped by the smell of warm cotton, a soft, enticing fragrance that Holly almost hated to leave when her mother made her request. "Lolli, I need you to go to town for a loaf of bread," she said.

Lolli was a nickname given to her by August's mother, Ida, a woman so sweet and full of love for her family that everyone felt compelled to follow her lead when it came to using pet names. Lolli, short for Lollipop, which had its origins in Holly—in other words, it was arrived at in a silly, roundabout manner that only Ida had understood.

Belle handed her a dime. "Come straight home, and mind not to squish the bread." As Holly lifted her coat off the hook by the door, her mother called after her, "And check the mail at the post office."

These solitary trips to town were a new thing for Holly. Her mother had decided recently, without explanation or fanfare, that she was ready. Holly's newfound freedom suddenly made the world a brighter, more interesting place.

Alone, without her mother or sister to distract her, she noticed everything.

She marched past the double-story red-brick grade school, square as a box, which both her father and mother had attended and where she was now in the fourth grade. A couple of kids she knew sailed high on one of the tall swing sets. Filled with the importance of her mission, Holly glanced their way as she passed but didn't lessen her pace.

Passing by her big-windowed classroom, Holly was reminded of the most embarrassing moment of her life, which she had suffered just this past month. She had been giving a book report in front of the class on *The Little Elephant*, a book she'd chosen herself. As she talked—her first time standing in a front of a class—a huge green bottle fly buzzed noisily around her head and landed on her face. She waved it away with her hand, only to have it land again in the same spot. All the kids laughed. She wasn't sure if they were laughing at her and her book report or at the fly and her vain attempts to shoo it away. What a *stupid* book to choose! A baby book, almost. What had she been thinking? Her face had burned with embarrassment, and more than anything she'd wanted a hole to open in the floor for her to fall into. Holly could feel her face turn hot now, just recalling the humiliating experience.

She willfully turned her attention away from her place of torture, as she'd come to think of the room, to the other side of the street, where a white clapboard two-story house surrounded by huge maples presided over the street corner. Under the roof eaves, gingerbread, elaborate in its design, trimmed the steep angling spaces. Holly longed to get a closer look at the grand old place, but she didn't dare step foot on the lawn. Margaret Angrove, stern-faced and wispy as a leaf rake, guarded her lawn fiercely. She was notorious for watching out the big windows of her house and then rushing onto the wrap-around porch to scream and wave her arms at any kid who trespassed on her yard.

Margaret sometimes cared for her brother, Perry, a tall, sinewy character who was off at Alton, the state lunatic asylum, more than he was at home. Just before he'd been carted to Alton the last time, Perry had pranced down the middle of the street on a perfectly clear sunny day, draped in a long, yellow rain slicker with a matching broad-rimmed rain hat, yelling angrily at kids passing on their bikes to get on home out of the rain. Holly had heard about it at school from the Skyler boys, whom Perry had confronted. *The old loony,* they'd said, laughing and imitating his long, stork-like step.

As she crossed the street, taking little skipping steps, it occurred to Holly that maybe she should feel sorry for the old woman. It couldn't be easy being Margaret Angrove. If, in the future, she saw Margaret outside in her yard or somewhere like the grocery store, she would say hello to her. Holly crossed her heart with her hand and hoped to die if she didn't keep her promise to herself. *Do unto others as you would have them do unto you.* The Golden Rule. Her mother had taught it to her.

On she walked, past two churches—the high-steepled First Christian Church, where she and her family belonged, and the brown-bricked, stained-glassed Universalist Church with its flat roof, perched solidly on its little knoll, where some of the teachers at Holly's school attended. "Fair-weather Christians" she'd heard the Universalists called, although she had no idea what it meant. When she'd asked, her mother had clicked her tongue and said people should be allowed to worship how they saw fit, without judgment or malice. "Judge not, lest ye be judged," her mother had said, quoting the Bible. *Millerville has five churches in all,* Holly thought, counting them on her fingers as she got closer to Main Street. *First Christian, First Baptist, Methodist, Church of Christ, Universalist.* "Don't it all boil down to the same thing?" her mother had said.

And then Main Street, where, in the matter of a step around the corner, Millerville transformed into something entirely different from quiet streets and empty weekday-afternoon churches.

Cars lined both sides of the street, parked at angles facing the businesses. People came and went, but there was no sense of hustle or bustle or unpleasantness. On the sidewalk in front of the barbershop, Holly heard, "Fine, fine," and then, "She's feelin' poor, but I thank you for askin'." Outside the J. I. Case dealership, amid the heady, burnt smell of old axle grease, one woman said to another, "The poor thing was plumb tore-up. Roy had to get out the rifle." It was Pam Goble's mother. Pam was in Holly's class; her father was a farmer and an elder at Holly's church. Holly would bet it was Pam's little dog, Clipper, who got the bullet. She would have to remember to tell Pam "Sorry about Clipper" at school tomorrow.

The grocery store was the usual obstacle course. One couldn't go there without having to get past Mr. Abel, the grocer. Today it was, "How, Holly!" He held up his right hand in his goofy version of an Indian greeting. She thought it was stupid and embarrassing and that he was making fun of her name somehow.

"Hello, Mr. Abel," she said, stopping in front of him only to be polite like her mother had taught her: *If you walk past people with nothing more than a hello, they'll think you're stuck up. You don't want to be thought of in that way, do you? So stop and talk. And stand up straight.* So she stood erect, her arms at her sides, giving Mr. Abel her full attention.

Mr. Abel looked a little ridiculous, in Holly's estimation. He had a narrow, pointed face like a deer, and he always walked fast, bent forward in the middle like he was in a race. He wore a white full apron, usually stained with blood from the meat counter. No matter how much she tried, Holly couldn't imagine her dad or her gramps in an apron.

"And how was school today, Holly?" he asked.

"Good," she said. Always the same questions; always the same answers.

"What grade are you in again?"

"Fourth grade."

"Mrs. Flanders."

"Yeah."

"How do you like Mrs. Flanders?"

"Fine. I like her a lot."

What he said next made Holly's legs go suddenly wobbly.

"What's your grandpa going to do once our new bridge is done?" he asked. He watched her face closely, like there might be more there than he would get in an answer. Holly had overheard her mother telling her father that Dan Abel knew everyone's business, and what he didn't know, he would try to find out. She suddenly felt an overwhelming dislike for Mr. Abel and his big fake smile.

Without thinking, she mumbled, "Mind your own business!"—a phrase she'd heard her gramps use when talking to his friend, Mr. Welch. She said it low but loudly enough that he heard it. She almost reached with her hand for something to steady herself, but she stood in the middle of the aisle. She felt shocked and a little scared—she had never, ever talked to an adult like that before. But she didn't regret saying it—no she didn't, not one bit, not even if she got in trouble for it later.

Mr. Abel's smile had disappeared. He had a stunned look on his face.

Sweetly now, Holly said, "Mr. Abel, my mom wants me to get a loaf of bread and hurry home." She could feel his eyes on her back as she hurried away from him.

Once away from Mr. Abel, the impact of what he had said about her gramps hit her. She knew work on the new bridge had started—her dad and mom talked about it. But it had never occurred to her, until now, that the ferry wouldn't just go on running as usual once the bridge was built.

Her gramps. The ferryboat. In her mind, they were like sunshine and blue sky, neither existing without the other. A sense of terrible doom flooded over her, like nothing she had ever experienced before. She felt sick. She stopped and leaned against the shelf in the cereal aisle to steady herself. And then she saw it: her gramps plunging into a black abyss. *Oh, Gramps, no. No! Gramps!*

CHAPTER 9

CARDINALS

John Welch sat by the window, reading the newspaper in Edna's favorite easy chair, her body's outline still imprinted on it as if she had only just left the room. Through the window glass he heard the *chip-chip* of a male cardinal to its mate. It was a call of profound alertness, the male protecting her, wanting to know where she was at all times, and that she was okay. Now and then the female chipped back to him—*I'm here; I'm right here.*

Edna had adored cardinals. "They mate for life, John," she'd said once, in awe. "Imagine that—birds, simple creatures, mating for life."

"Yes, dear, but they only live for three or four years," he answered.

She slapped at his arm. "You have it so rough," she said, giggling like a young girl.

Welch rattled his newspaper and turned to another page. The bird calls made him feel melancholy. With his wife gone two years now, who did he have that needed him in that way? Edna had depended on him, and he on her. Like the cardinals, they were devoted to one another. In the final sweep, though, he was not able to protect her. The female cancer had bested him, snuck up on both of them and laid her low before he could even fix his mind on the fact that she was not long for this world.

He watched the cardinals move on to the hickory grove across the gravel road from the house, where he still kept a few cows. The female led the way, her wings a blur. Then she tucked them to her sides and went into a quick downward arc. Another quick flurry of wings and she rose, forming the upward half of the arc, like an airplane stalling and restarting. The pattern was repeated over and over as she dwindled from view. The male's flight path was the same—a bustle of wings, the drop, the rise, the drop, the rise—fifty yards or so behind the female. "Keep up, old boy," Welch said aloud. He chuckled to himself and returned to his paper.

He was reading the *Gazette*'s weekly report on who'd had Sunday dinner with whom. No great revelations here. Martha Baker's married daughter, Adelaide, "traveling" on Sunday with her family from their farm a couple miles north of Millerville to have fried chicken with Martha in town. Pecan pie for dessert. Welch had sampled Martha's pecan pie. It, if nothing else, was worthy of mention. And then Mae Benson and her husband, Chester, hosting the Ramseys, Mildred and Harry, for cards on Saturday evening.

Dorothy Smith from the *Gazette* had stopped calling his house after Edna died. "I don't have company, and I don't want company, Dot," he had told her. Welch knew that Dorothy hated being called Dot—she considered it beneath her and too familiar. "You can call me as much as you want, but the answer will be the same, unless you consider Ralph Munday coming over to borrow my chainsaw newsprint-worthy." It was her nosiness that irked him more than anything—why she called, wanting to know if old John Welch was falling to pieces now that his wife was gone.

"Write about yourself, Dot," he'd said testily. "I, for one, would like to know what you and Wilbur have been up to. You never write about that. Do tell." Wilbur was a dandy, a native of Millerville. His parents had published the *Gazette*, and he had gone off to university in Chicago to find a wife worthy of him.

That comment put an end to the calls—that and the chainsaw remark, he reckoned.

Page four, the last page: Dorothy's piece on the bridge. Besides a short ditty about her "interview" with Floyd Bailey and what the citizens of Millerville could expect in the next few weeks, she editorialized on bridge versus ferry. "The time has come," she wrote. "A slow ferry plying the river is a romantic notion from another time. Millerville is now beyond that, being well positioned to become a major center of commerce."

The editorial went on in a similar vein, comparing what had happened in Terre Haute, forty miles up the river, to what could happen in Millerville. "While the rapid expansion of our northern neighbor couldn't be repeated in its exact form here, due to its close proximity, something of a less energetic but still ambitious sort is quite realistic and possible."

Lofty words and long, drawn-out sentences. Welch held no tolerance for Dorothy Smith. She was a stuffed bag of wind, filled to the brim with self-satisfaction. Even if what she said about it being time for a change from ferry to bridge was true, she seriously overestimated the effect a bridge would have on Millerville's economy. Things might pick up a bit, but a major center of commerce? He toyed with the idea of writing a letter to the editor but quickly dropped it. It would only encourage her.

What really got Welch's goat was the accompanying photograph—a picture of the ferry with the inglorious caption, "Millerville's Own Queen Mary," and in smaller print, "and Her King George V." In the picture, Shyrock stood, his back to the rail, looking distrustfully—and a little stunned—into the camera. It had just rained, and his newsboy cap drooped clownishly around his ears. His pants flagged over the tops of his high boots, and his old, wet coat, the threads loosened even more by rain, draped around him like a tent. He looked like a deflated balloon. It was mean-spiritedness, pure and simple.

Welch felt the blood rise into his neck. For nearly forty years, Buck had been the one who waited there at the riverside. If not actually at the ferry, he could be summoned from his simple house overlooking the landing with a single beep of the horn, or a shout, or failing that, a knock on the door at any hour of the day or night. Buck Shyrock was more reliable than the sun itself.

Because of its longstanding presence on the river, operated by three generations of Shyrocks, almost everyone in the two-state region knew about the ferry. Some in the Wabash Valley even forwent using the name Millerville when referring to the place and called it Shyrock's Ferry instead.

Buck lived for his work and, consequently, for the town.

"Goddamn it ta hell!" John Welch yelled, slamming the paper against the arm of the chair. How long would it take Shyrock to catch wind of this? Not long. Not in Millerville, where all news traveled fast, good or bad.

He might be a little ornery and rough around the edges, and yes, stuck in the past, but Buck Shyrock deserved better.

CHAPTER 10

GOING OUT ON A LIMB

Holly arrived home, breadless, without the mail, sweating inside her winter coat. Belle hurried to her as she stood motionless just inside the door, pale as a ghost, and felt her forehead.

"Holly, what's wrong?" she asked, stripping off her daughter's coat. "What happened?"

The girl muttered something but kept looking down at the floor.

"Something's happened," Belle persisted. "Tell me."

Holly averted her eyes when Belle tried to get her to look at her.

"You are soaked. Come into the bedroom and get out of those wet clothes."

In the girls' bedroom, little Vivian slipped in behind her mother. She stood silently and stared around Belle at her sister, instinctively knowing that this was a time, if there ever was one, to keep quiet.

"Oh, Holly, talk to Mommy." Belle pulled her close and held her. "You can tell me," she whispered into Holly's ear.

But Holly couldn't tell her something she didn't understand herself. She wanted to tell her mother—more than anything—what she'd seen in the grocery store. She couldn't bear not telling her; it was so horrible and terrifying.

She would have liked her mother to help her make sense of it, but she simply didn't have the words. She started to say "dark pit," but this wouldn't even begin to describe what she'd seen and felt. The mere thought of it made her shudder so hard in her mother's arms that talk was out of the question.

Belle laid fresh clothes on Holly's bed. "You sit right here, and I'll get you a bath ready," she said, patting the edge of the bed. Turning, she nearly plowed over Vivian. "Sweetie, go back to your puzzles in the kitchen. Your sister will be okay." She gave her a nudge. "Go."

The child slipped away, for once doing as she was told without it having to be repeated.

When the tub was full, Belle went back to retrieve Holly. She found her lying sideways on the bed in her underclothes, asleep. Her mouth was open, a spot of saliva soaking into the quilt, and her feet still draped over the side. Belle stood her up to pull back the blankets, and Holly jerked violently, her free arm shooting out to her side like she was trying to catch herself. "My poor baby," Belle cooed to her daughter and covered her with the blankets.

Without waking, Holly snuggled into the blankets and pillow like a small animal burrowing into its cozy nest. Thus settled, she didn't move again all night.

When she woke the next morning, the stunned look returned to her face. Holly asked her mother if she could stay home from school.

"Yes, you certainly may," Belle answered, straightening the bedclothes. "What can I get you? Hot chocolate sound good?"

"Um . . . no thanks. Could I have a glass of water please?" Holly smiled weakly—apologetically—at her mother. "I love you, Mommy. I'm sorry."

"I love you too, Lolli. There's nothing to be sorry for, sweetheart."

Belle could tell from the look on her face that Holly wasn't ready to talk about whatever had happened on her errand to town. Past experience had taught Belle that if her daughter didn't want to talk about something, no amount of cajoling or sternness would get her to open up.

≈ ≈ ≈

The evening before, when August came in from work, Belle had told him what had happened. After peeking in on Holly, he'd said, "It's odd. What does she have to upset her?"

"There are many things in this world to disturb a child," Belle answered. "We can't protect her from everything, though we might think we can." Belle thought of Holly's reaction to her grandmother's death: she'd cried inconsolably for a week. Telling Holly, "Grams is in heaven now," didn't help. "But I'll never see her again" was all Holly could say. "Never ever." Weren't children supposed to be unable to grasp the finality of death?

"If you haven't noticed," Belle continued, "Holly is a very sensitive child. She picks up everything, like lint to a cloth. She knows things before we do."

"Yes, she is sensitive—too sensitive sometimes, I agree," August said.

"I didn't say *too* sensitive—"

"But 'knowing things'?" he interrupted. "I think you're going out on a limb there."

"I'm not!" Belle turned away from him. August stood in the middle of the kitchen, pronouncing his doubts, as if the dust and dirt on his coat, picked up from the world outside the sheltered domesticity of the home, gave him special authority to pass judgment.

"Supper will be something simple and quick. And we don't have any bread."

"I could have stopped."

"Only if you could predict the future," she said, suddenly disgusted with him. "Go clean up, please." She busied herself at the icebox so she wouldn't have to watch him leave the room.

CHAPTER 11

A SINGLE TEAR IN THE CORNER OF HIS EYE

Will Turner came from a long line of hard drinkers, brawlers, and ne'er-do-wells. Growing up, little Billy, the oldest of a roguish, ragtag mob scattered in ages, as if to prove the span of the human fertility period, somehow always caught the brunt of his old man's rage. When anything didn't go well, as it often did not, when "everythin' turned to shit," as his daddy proclaimed loudly and often, someone had to be blamed. More often than not, in this fractured, foul-mouthed, gut-smacked family, that someone was Billy.

Abuse of Billy's mother and of the children was plain enough: round black bruises and long, livid stripes, some fading to purple and then red, followed by green and finally pale yellow. A rainbow of misery, there for the world to see. For the boys, black eyes and cauliflower ears. The girls—bruises, yes, and worse still, other abuses that were only rumored at among the townspeople. Sometimes, when it got especially bad and the continuous yelling at the far, brushy end of High Street could no longer be ignored, the county sheriff was called. But all he got was denials from everyone, mother and children included.

For the sheriff and his "lap dogs," the entire Turner clan held a special hatred. The law was the most to blame for the Turners' many problems. It was because of them—and the judge and the lawyers, all of them "crooked as a pig dick"—that Old Man Turner went to the penal farm for manslaughter. "The dumb bastard shoulda pulled his car further off the road to change his damn tire," he told his family. Never mind that Turner had been sitting in the Old York Tavern that entire day before the crime happened that evening.

Each time the sheriff visited the Turner place, the yelling would at least subside for a while.

For Billy—and Billy alone—there was the occasional broken bone. The town doctor, Jeb Singleton, would send out for the sheriff and then set the broken bone while Billy grimaced and cursed, a single tear gathering in the corner of one eye but never falling. His mother, Gladys Turner, standing stiff-lipped and reticent in the corner, would be sent out of the room.

For the sheriff, nothing: "I toldja already. I fell outta a tree."

"You don't have to put up with this, ya know, son," the sheriff told him.

Billy ducked under the sheriff's hand, coming for the shoulder of his good arm. "Go ta hell," he muttered.

So when Billy grew into young Will ("Don't fuckin' call me *Billy*—I ain't your fuckin' baby"), his need to steal gas had an explanation outside of himself: "That goddamned McNutt has plenty o' money, the rich som'bitch. He even pays someone to run his ferry for him. He won't miss a gallon here and a gallon there."

Buck Shyrock began noticing that the steel fuel tank kept at the top of the landing was emptying quicker than usual.

Used to be, a full tank would last for a month and a half, two months. It dwindled down to a month and then three weeks. As Will Turner got bolder, thinking it was easier than he expected to hoodwink Old Man Shyrock—"the old fool, he deserves it. He makes it so easy"—Buck began staying up at night to watch.

He hadn't waited long when on the second night of sitting up beside the partially open window, he heard shuffling in the gravel over by the fuel tank. It was pitch-black outside, a moonless, cloudy night. A light breeze blew, soughing through the bare tree limbs. And then the clank of hard metal against the hollowness of an empty gas can.

Quickly, Buck slid open the window and aimed his hand lamp toward the sound. Turner froze, staring back at the blinding beam of light like a thieving raccoon caught raiding the trash bin. Panicking, he cut and ran, leaving the fuel spout and hose snaked on the hard ground, the dented gas can abandoned.

The sheriff was called in the next morning. Besides Shyrock's identification, it didn't help Turner's cause that at the bottom of the gas can was scratched in jagged but readable letters, *LT.* Lucas Turner, the old man.

But when young Will was carted off to jail, someone else had to be blamed. The ferry operator was to catch the brunt of it.

LOG ENTRY: 20 January, 1939. Today I inspected the material taken from the test holes and began a log, classifying the different materials encountered in drilling these holes.

Satisfactory test holes were drilled by a small portable rig with a light drop hammer and rotary drilling machinery. A casing was driven from 3 feet to 20 feet and then washed out by a pressure pump mounted on a rig. Very few dry samples were taken because much of the material was a coarse sand or fine gravel and would not hold in the sampler. All washings were examined closely, and the log was made from these observations. On reaching rock, the rotary drilling machinery was fitted with a diamond-pointed core drill, and cores were taken from 3 feet to 17 feet. Firm shale was found under the west abutment and west pier, at 5 feet and 25 feet below low-water elevation. Under the other foundations, the shale was 59 feet to 63 feet below low-water elevation.

After a careful study of the boring data, it was evident to me that ten of the foundations were unsatisfactory as designed because they were founded in very sandy material, and the proposed elevation for the bottom of these foundations was as much as 15 feet above the lowest elevation of the main channel, where any shifting of the channel would undermine them and cause complete failure.

The west abutment foundation was satisfactory as designed, since it was founded on a stratum of sandy gravel with sufficient bearing capacity for carrying the load and was located back from the river, where there was no danger of it being undermined.

I suggested increasing the depth for the other ten foundations, and the bridge commissioner's engineer readily agreed, since the original design had been made before the boring data was available.

From my observations of the driving of the steel casings used in the test boring, I also suggested that all steel piling would have to extend to rock to secure the necessary bearing capacity. This suggestion was carried out in the two heavier foundations, but the bridge commissioner's engineer thought we might be able to secure the necessary bearing by using 70-foot piles for the viaduct bents and 50-foot piles for the east abutment foundation.

CHAPTER 12

A PERFECT BALANCE

Despite his genuine concern over Shyrock, Welch couldn't keep himself away from Floyd Bailey and talk of the bridge-building project. All through high school, Welch had planned to go to college to study engineering. He had been accepted to the University of Illinois, but in the spring of his high school senior year, the Panic of 1893 struck the nation. Crop prices plummeted. With the future far from certain, his father retracted his promise to pay for his schooling. Welch, dejected but realistic about his prospects, joined the navy instead.

His early conversations with Floyd were of soundings and test borings and steel casings. Light drop hammers, diamond-point core drills, and rotary drills. Pressure pumps and boring data. Coarse sand, fine gravel, sandy gravel, firm shale. Low-water elevation, main channel lowest elevation, and undermining. Main pier footings and anchor footings. Viaduct bent piles, steel pier bents, and anchor bents. Concrete jackets. I-beams and H-beams. Cofferdam frames. Foundations. Stiff-leg derricks.

John Welch knew sand, he knew gravel, and he even knew a thing or two about shale. He fancied himself as having an understanding of foundations, at least in theory. But he grasped little else of what Floyd talked about.

Floyd was a fluid conversationalist, so he didn't seem to mind Welch's ignorance. In fact, in talking to the old farmer and encouraging him to ask questions, he claimed that he worked out several problems that he knew he would encounter in the days to come. Welch liked to think it was his small contribution to the building of the Millerville bridge.

Floyd told Welch that during his nine years as project engineer for the Department of Transportation, he had worked on several bridge projects, but this one was a new type of structure: a self-anchoring suspension bridge. The design, Floyd explained one morning at breakfast, talking between bites of food, was dictated by the depth of sand on the Indiana riverbank. There was nothing but sugar sand going to seventy-five feet below the surface. "Pouring a concrete foundation that far down would cost a fortune and was quickly ruled out," he said, glancing sideways at Welch as he dragged his toast through egg yolk. "The self-anchoring design was the logical alternative. A marvel of engineering, really."

Floyd's explanation went something like this: Following Newton's law that to every action there's an equal and opposite reaction, the first action would be the weight of the bridge deck itself (dead load) and the traffic that crossed it (live load), transmitted through the suspender cables to the main support cables as a pulling force. Because of the restrictions imposed by the Indiana bank, on this particular bridge the balancing "reaction" would take place on the Illinois side. At the end of the main cables that arched down from the seventy-foot tower on the Illinois bank, cable anchors would connect to horizontal steel beams, called stiffening girders, on either side of the bridge. The stiffening girders were manufactured to contain compressive force. This compressive force would counteract the pull, or tensile force, coming from the main suspension cables that carried the bridge's live and dead loads.

Seeing the confused look on Welch's face, Floyd laid down his fork, quickly wiped his fingers on a napkin, and fished for a pencil stub buried at the bottom of his shirt pocket. He brushed lint and bits of dirt off it and then pulled a fresh napkin out of the chrome container in front of him. He flattened the napkin on the counter and drew a picture with three arrows, all starting at a single point. One arrow pointed to the right at a forty-five degree angle, illustrating the pulling force of the main suspension cables. A second arrow pointed horizontally to the right, indicating the equivalent compressive force of the stiffening girder that traveled back toward the main body of the bridge deck and, in doing so, helped support it. The third, shorter arrow traveled straight up from the common point. "Because of this dynamic balancing of forces," Floyd said, clearly excited by the mere thought of it, "small, simple bridge supports attached to the ends of the two stiffening girders and mounted to the top of the Illinois abutment receive what little remains of the pulling force of the cables.

"There you have it—a self-supporting suspension bridge. Complex, yet simple," he concluded, dropping his pencil stub back into his shirt pocket with a flourish. "Isaac Newton was one hell of an engineer."

"It's complex all right. Not so sure about simple," Welch said, scratching his head where the white hair had been matted by his hat, which now hung on the coatrack by the door.

"Like most things, it all boils down to balance. When a perfect balance isn't maintained," Floyd said, "things go haywire." As if to illustrate his point, he ripped the napkin in half and dropped it into his empty plate where the egg yolk had been wiped mostly clean.

During the quiet that followed, Welch thought that up to this point in their conversations, neither of them had mentioned the ferry or that first day when Welch had caught Floyd's eye, and they had exchanged greetings. As though following Welch's train of thought, Floyd stared at the torn napkin in his plate with a faraway look on his face.

Finally, he said, "I took the ferry a few times with my family when I was a kid. I remember the old man—he seemed old even then, at least to me. He looked grumpy, but he wasn't—not really. He treated me like an honored guest. Showed me how the ferry worked."

"That'd be Shyrock. Stephen Shyrock. He's been operating that old raft for some forty years. Loves kids."

"Yes, Shyrock's Ferry," Floyd said, nodding his head. And then after a moment: "What will he do? I mean, once the bridge is completed."

Welch shrugged his shoulders and pursed his lips. He didn't have an answer, although he wished he did.

"It won't be easy," Floyd said quietly, real concern in his voice.

"No," Welch said. "That it won't."

"Wish I could help somehow."

"Don't know what that would be. I've wondered the same thing myself. And I've known him my whole life."

Welch asked himself again what Shyrock would say if he could see him now, sitting with the bridge's project engineer. In the enemy camp. There was no telling what he would say. Maybe nothing. Maybe he already knew about Welch's almost daily breakfast ritual. Buck could keep things to himself better than any man Welch had ever known. Sometimes, he was as taciturn as a rock.

He should tell him. It wasn't like it was a secret. But actually doing it was a different matter. Just the same, he told himself he would—he would tell Buck. The sooner, the better.

"Well, anyway," Floyd said, dropping money on the counter and gathering himself up, "remember what I said. If there's a way I can help, I'll do it."

Welch didn't have the heart to tell him he'd be seen as the adversary. Shyrock was as likely to accept aid from him as he would from, say, Dorothy Smith, whom he detested for her snooty ways.

"Thanks, Floyd. I will remember it."

≈ ≈ ≈

A goodly portion of the townspeople showed up to watch the maiden hole being dug. When the clam bucket, rigged to a derrick, took its first bite of riverbank, a hearty cheer went up. Then people started filtering away, and after a time only the old-timers remained—retired men with the spirit of labor still rattling around in their bones. They stood well back from the real action but listened to every shout and every order. They watched every move and grimace of the workmen and felt every strain of their arms and legs and backs in their own slack muscles.

For fear of being spotted somehow by Shyrock, Welch was not among them.

LOG ENTRY: 24 January, 1939. Excavation for the west main pier commenced today. The riverbank was leveled off just above water elevation so a cofferdam frame can be set up as a guide for the metal sheeting. The sky looks menacing and the river seems jittery in its movement. Just standing by it, you can sense a change in the air.

CHAPTER 13

MEN OF THE FUTURE

One morning, after Floyd had taken his leave, Welch walked out of the drugstore, past the front of the hardware store, and around the corner to the place where preliminary scratches in the brown dirt signaled the beginnings of the bridge approach and its connection with the existing road. Workers were gathering by the construction shack, their day's work not yet begun.

Fifty feet or so back from the river, a rectangular area was staked off, and there were small round mounds in the dirt where the bridge crew had done its test borings. *This is the spot,* Welch thought, *the fulcrum point where all the weight, all the tension and compression, and whatever else Floyd Bailey had mentioned would culminate—* the final action (or "reaction," according to Newton) of a modern, self-anchoring, steel suspension bridge. A perfect balance, Floyd had said. Balance, a delicate thing, even in steel and concrete—perhaps *especially* in steel and concrete. He felt humbled and in awe of men like Floyd Bailey, who could take concrete and long stretches of steel beams and wire cable and dangle it in thin air. As precarious and fragile as a spider web was how it all seemed to Welch. They were men of the future, Floyd Bailey and those like him.

Hard against the river, a twelve-foot-square section of riverbank had been excavated to just above water level. Here,

Welch knew, the west main pier of the bridge would stand—the tower reaching into the sky above the river, higher than any tree or building or hill in Millerville's history.

Before heading back to his truck parked on Main Street, Welch lifted his face to the darkened sky and sniffed the air. The river, he noticed, had that scheming look about it that Shyrock had talked about. Like it held a secret that would be revealed soon enough, when it was ready, but not until then.

Rain was coming, that was for certain. And it looked to be a doozey.

LOG ENTRY: 25 January, 1939. Overnight, rain mixed with snow fell, and the river began to rise before the cofferdam frame could be set. In order not to delay the work, timber piles were driven outside each corner of the foundation to support the frame above the rising water.

CHAPTER 14

THAT NIGGLING IN HIS BELLY

It started in earnest—without preliminaries, without rumblings—a torrent of heavy rain mixed with snow that plummeted straight down into the river as if returning home after a long journey.

A few days before the deluge started, Buck had cleaned and adjusted the steer boat's carburetor, blown out the fuel line, and replaced the spark plug, even though under normal circumstances it would have lasted much longer. He'd even taken the extra time needed to work out the bit of play in the throttle cable. For months he had been bothered by a lull in the motor's initial acceleration. With the rising, spruced-up current, he knew what was coming. Every second counted.

Waiting at the landing while Buck tinkered with the cable, a patron asked him what he was doing. "Gettin' 'er ready," Buck responded without looking up from his work. He recognized the gravelly voice of the parts runner from the Ford garage who made frequent trips to Terre Haute. Henry Hodges mostly sat around on the showroom floor, chain-smoking and talking to anyone who would listen. He and Old Man Farley, the Ford dealer, shared swigs from a bottle that Farley kept hidden in the soda pop cooler. Buck felt no need to hurry on Henry's account.

"Ready for what?" Henry persisted. He stood leaning against the hood of his car, not sorry for the chance to loaf, to stand and gaze out over the river.

"The flood that's headin' thissa way."

Henry pushed his hat back off his forehead and looked up at the sky and its scattered wispy clouds. He shifted his gaze upriver as though he half expected a sudden wall of water to appear from the opening in the trees where the riverbed made its final turn before passing by Millerville.

Folks in Millerville, Hodges included, had seen Buck be right about the weather enough times that they had learned not to doubt him. Some said he saw it in the sky when there were no signs obvious to anyone else. Some said he read it in the river's current, days, even weeks, before the rain started. Some believed he could feel the approach of rain stirring in the waters of his own body. This time, when the word got around town via Henry Hodges that Buck Shyrock was predicting a flood, some even said the ferry operator had summoned the rains to stop progress on the bridge.

Now that the rain had started, it didn't let up. The sky darkened and then darkened some more. Buck, of course, wasn't surprised, but he also didn't expect it to keep on the way it did. Within a few days, the river was well over its banks at the lower, Indiana side, crowding the top of the mound levee that followed along the back of the tree line. Out in the main current, it raced by—twisting, turning, corkscrewing, and somersaulting over itself—slathering with so much froth and foam that it appeared to have gone completely and irretrievably mad.

People flocked to the Millerville bank, gawking and pointing from within the dry shelter of their automobiles.

For those old enough to remember, the flood of 1913 came to mind, when many of the houses in Millerville stood in two to three feet of water. "Lost my corncrib in that one," one old farmer recalled. "They found it, ass over teakettle, down by Miller Creek."

As the swollen mass shot past, the watchers involuntarily smoothed the soles of their shoes against their floorboards, reassuring themselves that firm footing remained. How could there be so much water all at once? Where did it all come from? At the same time, they were proud of their wild, misbehaving Wabash. What did anyone else in the county, especially those snobs in Robinson, who always were calling them "river rats," have to compare with *this*?

Buck surrendered to its fury. He winched the ferry back away from the river and, as an extra precaution, off the flooded landing approach, so it was out of harm's way. He moored it to a boulder that had been dropped there for that purpose years ago by his father, during a previous flood. All he could do now was to wait for the rain to stop, for the river to crest, and for it to begin its slow retreat, as it always did.

As the river rampaged and several homes and businesses became inundated by water, the people of the town grew edgy. With the ferry out of commission, even if they had no reason to cross the river, they felt vulnerable, like a balance had been tipped precipitously. An escape route was closed off to them and only the return of the ferry could right it. As if to demonstrate how out of kilter their world had become, the river spilled onto the north end of Main Street, and Harold Abbott and Boots Myer had their picture snapped in Boots's johnboat out front of Dyson's Garage. It appeared in the *Gazette* the following day. What next? The Millerville ferry dry-docked, while a johnboat motored up and down Main Street!

Despite the rain and the flooded streets, drenched villagers began showing up at Buck's door. "How long d'you think it'll keep up?" they asked him. And, "Can't stay at this pace much longer, huh, Buck?" The ferry operator couldn't answer them. When the sky was chock-full of rain, it was hard to say when it would stop.

At the post office, Dorothy Smith from the *Gazette* approached Buck from behind. "No offense meant, Mr. Shyrock," she said to his back, forgoing any kind of greeting, "but a year from now when the bridge is completed, we won't have this problem." Edgy from too much sitting around, Buck turned on her before he had a chance to sort through his thoughts. He knew Dorothy well enough to know offense was exactly what she meant.

He had seen the picture of himself and the ferry. "Pretty clever, huh, Shyrock?" the person who passed him the paper had said. Buck had almost flung the paper into the river without making comment, but he remembered his better self. His face darkened as he folded the paper and handed it back to its owner. A quiet, unintelligible grunt was his only response. "Well, you have to admit it's pretty clever," the man said. Buck hadn't delivered this passenger with his customary smoothness. The ferry apron dug itself a hole in the Hoosier sand, and the previously bemused man was very nearly forced to use his kneecaps as landing gear.

Buck hadn't so much as glanced at the article. He saw the caption: *Millerville's Own Queen Mary (and Her King George V)*, and he couldn't help but see the headline in bold print: *Its Time Has Passed.* Buck would never forgive her for it.

Until being handed the paper, Buck hadn't realized how down in the cuffs the old ferry looked.

Now, at the post office, Buck faced off with his assailant. "Dorothy, don't be . . . don't . . . you don't know what you're talkin' 'bout," he said, stumbling over his own tongue.

"Well, of course I do. I'm simply saying one could take a bridge right over the river and in a fraction of the time it takes a ferry, regardless of the river's stage."

"Time! A fraction of the time!" Buck spat it out, as if viler words did not exist. "Ya talk about it like it's somethin' can only be parsed out on paper."

"Yes, a fraction of the time," Dorothy said again, resolute but puzzled just the same by his reaction.

"You don't know what a bridge'll do to this town," he said.

"Do to this town! Improve commerce, for starters," she sniffed. She looked him up and down, at his rough, grease-stained, baggy coat; his trousers, scuffed and bagged out over his boots; his tattered hat. Black hairs sprouted like spike grass out of big ears that lay flat against his head. She sniffed again. "And maybe—just maybe—pull it out of the nineteenth century and into the twentieth."

Buck straightened up to his full height and adjusted his cap. This snooty woman might have been raised and college educated in Chicago, while he was forced out of school early to help out on the ferry, but she wasn't going to tell him what was good for Millerville. He snorted. "Greed. That's what it's about, ain't it? Money. More money. That's all 'at matters to you and those like ya."

"I don't consider commerce synonymous with greed."

"Commerce!" Buck scoffed. "You build your bridge, and there won't be as much commerce as there was before.

People will pass right on through Millerville with barely a blink of an eye. Those already here will find more reason—reasons they never even thought of before—to leave and do their tradin' somewheres else." *And there's the river,* he thought. *The river they'll pass clean over, encased in their automobiles, barely aware of its presence down below.* He didn't waste his breath on that part. Dorothy Smith was one of those fussy birds who never set foot out of her car when crossing on the ferry.

Dorothy raised her nose, narrowed her eyes, and studied him for a moment longer, as if she was surprised he actually had a cogent thought. "You have your opinion, Mr. Shyrock, and I have mine," she said. She spun on her heel and made an exit, her nose nearly brushing cobwebs off the ceiling.

Walking home, Buck replayed the confrontation in his mind. Well, he had stood up to that fancy-pants newspaper lady all right. Held his own, hadn't he? But there was no satisfaction in the thought, only a cool hollowness in his chest, a niggling in his belly. Even the hound, loping behind the agitated Shyrock to keep up, couldn't get him to proffer a pat on the head.

When Buck rounded the corner next to the Ford garage and spotted a car parked at the edge of the flooded landing—its tires touching the water and the driver pacing outside—he forgot all about Dorothy Smith and her talk of so-called progress.

"There you are!" the man said, walking toward Buck at a savage pace.

"And what of it?" Buck responded testily, not liking the fellow's superior, demanding tone. He thought the man might trample right over him, so he drew up short and waited.

"I have to cross the river! I have to—right now!" the man said once he reached him. His breath smelled of liquor; his veined, bloodshot eyes nearly bugged out of his face.

"Have you took a good look?" Buck asked him. From where they stood, their feet were almost level with the frightful-looking current that passed by them like a landslip moving on its own separate plane.

The man's face wasn't familiar. He had drooping bags under his eyes and except for the wildness of his eyes, he looked as if he could use a good long rest. His blondish hair had been doused with tonic and combed back at some earlier, brighter point in the day—there was still evidence of a comb mark here, a coiffed wave there—but mostly it drooped sadly down around his ears. Buck wondered about the fellow's sanity.

"Hang the river! You *must* take me across!"

"Mister, I'm plumb outta commission. I ain't afraid of a little high water, but this ain't the same. If the river didn't come over the top of us, the runnin' cable would surely snap, and no tellin' what would happen then." Buck pointed across to where the current raced through the tops of the willows and butted against the bigger trees like it was determined to thrust them out of its path. "Prob'ly we'd get hung up in those trees over yonder," he continued, trying to convince the man. "It'd bust the boat into toothpicks for certain. And us with it."

The man shifted impatiently from one leg to the other, unable to stand still. "Then I'll do it myself!" he yelled, once he realized Shyrock couldn't be swayed. With that, he rushed to the ferryboat and began thrusting and heaving against its bulky frame with his arms and a shoulder, grunting like a mad ox.

"I think the poor feller's let go his faculties," Buck said to Rebel, who sat on her haunches, looking from the man to Shyrock and then back again, as if expecting Buck to explain this strange turn of events.

Buck waited for the man to expend himself. Once the inevitable happened and the man dropped to his knees, heaving for breath, Buck cautiously approached him.

"Why ya feelin' such a need ta git across the river, son?" Buck had begun to feel a little sorry for him. He figured anyone who would try what he just had deserved a little understanding.

Still resting on his knees and gripping the corner of the ferry for support, the man looked up at Shyrock with what could only be interpreted as evil intent. "To hell with you and your damn ferry," he growled. "You're as useless as tits on a boar."

Shyrock took no particular offense at the man's unflattering description of him. *I kinda agree with him,* he thought. *These last long days, I've been nothin' but useless.* Buck wasn't sure where it would end if he didn't get back to work soon.

The man didn't wait for a response. He jumped to his feet, his previous energy suddenly returning. Still panting, he stumbled around his car, flung himself in behind the wheel, and spun the car around backwards until it faced the opposite direction. After flashing Shyrock the bird, he was gone in a spray of gravel. Rocks peppered the ferry. One stone grazed Buck's hat and another, his ear. He stood, rubbing the ear, looking at the wet, glistening tire marks the man left all the way to Main Street. The drenching rain had already begun erasing them.

"That about describes it. Useless as tits on a boar," he said, turning his unharmed ear toward the river, listening for something, anything, to encourage him a little. That earlier morning in the fog, just before he spotted the stranger standing on the Indiana bank, was the last time the river had spoken to him. It *sang* to him, is what it had done, its voice strong and beautiful. Never before, until that morning, had the river sung to him. Now, all he heard was the rain sloshing against the already saturated ground.

LOG ENTRY: 9 February, 1939. The river rose so suddenly, all work had to be ceased entirely. The cofferdam frame is entirely covered. Before it could be moved out of harm's way, some equipment on the low east bank was inundated by the rising waters. Time will tell if it has been rendered unusable. Delivery of all other equipment and construction steel is postponed.

I've never seen anything quite like it—the suddenness with which the river rose. The old ferryman, like a protective hen, pulled his precious ferry to the top of the landing.

The rain stopped and so did the river's rising. After it crested at well above flood stage, it began to drop, little by little each day. First, Buck winched the ferry fully back into the littered, scummy water, befouled by all the detritus the river had picked up while out of its banks. As the water receded, Buck eased out more cable from the boulder.

Finally, the ferry was afloat in its heavy, cumbersome way at its customary station off the end of the landing, and Buck, except for the persistent niggling in his gut, was back to his old self, even humming snappy little tunes from his school days. He posted a sign next to Main Street, replacing the "Ferry Closed" board with one that read "Ferry Back."

The citizenry of Millerville breathed a collective sigh of relief, feeling not as out of sorts as when their ferryboat had lain on the bank like a beached behemoth. Of course, they had all read Dorothy Smith's article, but unlike the opinionated and snooty Dorothy, they would miss the old ferry once the bridge was built. They couldn't help it. It was as much a part of them as the village was. What they wouldn't miss, though, was that nagging feeling of vulnerability and uncertainty every time the river escaped its banks. Imagine it! A bridge that was immune to all the river's vagaries and wild moods. "Progress" was the word rolling off everyone's tongue.

LOG ENTRY: 20 February, 1939. Back to work. The changes in design previously mentioned were worked out during the flood break. The contractor cleaned and checked equipment that had been caught in the flood waters. Luckily, any damage done was repairable, and the cleaning and mechanical work was carried out as quickly as possible. Today, the contractor unloaded and rigged more equipment. He tells me he is ready to begin actual construction.

Originally, the derrick on the west bank was to complete the west main pier and abutment and to handle structural steel on the west bank. The derrick on the east was to complete the anchor pier and drive the viaduct bent piles and then complete the east abutment. The east derrick was then to be used to erect the structural steel.

As with most construction jobs, the original plan has been changed, in this case due to the very real possibility of another flood covering the east bank. The delivery point for the structural steel is now the west bank, and the order of erection has been changed in favor of the west. The west derrick will be used to erect the structural steel.

CHAPTER 15

NOTHIN' GOOD

Work on the bridge commenced anew. On the Illinois bank there was a flurry of activity. Incessant pounding rattled Buck's windows in their frames. Where the landing jutted out from the bank, creating a pool of stalled water, the surface hopped in concentric circles. Buck had never witnessed this kind of motion on the river's face. It was unsettling to him after all his years on the river.

Despite the disturbances of bridge building, ferrying went on, if not in its usual relaxed manner then at least as a conveyance of people and their goods from one side of the river to the other. No longer did people simply stand out on the deck, stretching their legs and taking in the fresh air and the scenic river. Now, all talk was of the bridge. Buck's fares began pumping him for information, peering over where workers moved about on the banks, intent on their digging and drilling and loud pounding. Buck continued to look straight ahead, pretending not to hear their questions over the motor.

The current still carried debris left over from the flood. Occasionally, tree trunks as big around as barrels floated downriver, menacing in the way they stayed submerged, just out of sight, and then appeared suddenly to reveal their hazardous bulk.

At first, Buck thought he'd hit one of these drift logs with the propeller, but looking behind the steer boat through the cloudy scrim of water, he spotted hair . . . and below that, clothes. To make sure he wasn't seeing something not actually there—that the river wasn't up to its old trick of making things appear different from they were in reality— he blinked his eyes, hoping a log would be a log when he reopened them. But it was what it had first appeared to be: a carcass. A human carcass.

Rebel took to sniffing the air. Upon spotting the body, she catapulted to the deck. Tail tucked between her legs, she slinked to the far end of the ferry and stood there, head down and skulking, watching Buck out of the corner of her eye.

Buck cut the motor and quickly reached to his left over the starboard side of the ferry. He grabbed a long hickory pole that he kept there in case it was ever needed as a lifesaving device. Mainly, he'd used it for fishing worthwhile items out of the river. Once, he'd retrieved a bicycle floating upside down, buoyed by its still-inflated tires. Another time, a wooden porch swing, chains and all, which he'd handed over to August and Belle. This time the river's offering was of a more sobering variety.

"What do you have there, Shyrock?" his sole passenger inquired from the deck, craning his neck to see.

"Nothin' good," Buck answered and went to work with his pole. He poked around until he hooked the poor drowned soul's belt. He ran the pole on through until he had enough purchase to force the body backward into the current and alongside the ferry's stern. By this time, the passenger had moved to the back of the ferry to have a look.

"Grab him, will ya?" Buck grunted, straining mightily against the opposing force of the water. The body was waterlogged and unbelievably heavy.

The passenger's mouth gaped. "No way am I touching that thing!"

"It's not a thing!" Buck shouted. "Now grab ahold o' him like I told ya!" The man, decked out in a wool suit and tie, an expensive top coat, a fine hat, and polished cap-toed boots, just stood there. "All right, then, come here and take this pole! I'll pull him out myself!"

Reluctantly, the man did as he was ordered.

Buck lowered the rearward apron to water level. He got down on his knees and tugged and pulled until the body was on the deck next to him.

The gentleman, still holding fast to the pole that protruded through the dead person's belt, took one look at the horrible, bloated mess that had once been alive and heaved the pole away, as if the stink and rot were quickly making their way up the pole's length toward him. He doubled over the side of the steer boat and emptied his breakfast into the river.

$$\approx \approx \approx$$

Word traveled quickly. First the county sheriff came, then the coroner, and then the local undertaker. Of course, a curious and lively contingent of the townsfolk had already shown up but thankfully, not before Shyrock had dug out the tarp he kept in a small shed at the top of the landing. With it, he covered the sordid, catfish- and turtle-nibbled remains.

The sheriff, after covering his nose and mouth with his handkerchief, raised one side of the tarp and quickly gave the corpse the once-over. He then refolded the hanky, taking care that it was done just so, and returned it to its pocket. Next, he continued his investigation by interrogating Buck in the following manner: When did you first see the body? What did you do next? Do you recognize the deceased? Is there any reason to suspect foul play? Is there anything else you haven't mentioned? How did the passenger react?

"He wretched," Buck answered, fairly well disgusted with the sheriff's vapid line of questioning. "Sorry, but the current done took it away."

The sheriff, his thick mustache twitching from Buck's insolence, was astute enough to recognize his questioning of the ferryboat operator had reached the limits of its usefulness.

"That will be all," the sheriff said, as though dismissing Buck from his own landing.

Buck glowered at him but held his tongue.

Before the Crawford County coroner could finish his grisly task, a thin, pale, bespectacled man, calling himself the "chief coroner" of Sullivan County, Indiana, arrived on the scene from across the way in a commandeered fisherman's johnboat, with the fisherman himself at the helm. The gentleman, already in the vicinity when he heard the news, demanded to know what the deuce was going on.

Once it was determined unequivocally, with the testimony of the still green-gilled passenger, that Shyrock had indeed hauled the poor dead man out of the water closer to the Illinois side (the state line being in the middle of the river), the coroner from the wrong side of the Wabash harrumphed himself back into the johnboat and returned to his home state, standing aloft and looking every bit like General George Washington crossing the Delaware, sans uniform and fancy hat.

Rebel, having recovered somewhat from her case of nerves, watched him go. She let go a single, unfriendly bark, as if to say, *And don't come back.*

"Damn fool'll fall inta the river hisself if he ain't careful," the Crawford County coroner said, shaking his head. "Just as long as it's nearer the Hoozier bank," he said, putting emphasis on the misplaced *z*. "Got my hands full enough here."

August showed up toward the end of the fiasco. "Dad, you okay?" he asked, his hand reaching out and almost touching his father's elbow. Shyrock's look was one of pale confusion, something the son hadn't seen on his father's firm, taciturn face since his mother died.

"I'm fine," Buck said. "Yeah, fine." He removed his hat, a rare thing when outside his own house, revealing his mostly bald pate. He scraped the back of his hand over his dry mouth. He had been thinking of the fellow he'd dealt with at the flooded ferry landing who wanted transport across the swollen river. What had become of him? He knew that the drowned man wasn't the same person—not the same hair color, and the tattered, muddy clothes were different. But spotting the decomposed body had put him into a state of bewilderment, like he was somehow responsible for the other man's fate because he hadn't done enough to dissuade him from his mad desire to cross the river (although for the life of him, he couldn't imagine what he could have done differently). To Shyrock's mind, the two—the disturbed man and the drowned one—were connected somehow. On the river, everything was connected—past, present, and future. And everything that happened, Shyrock believed—as his father had believed and his father before him—happened for a reason. "Not always clear why at the time," his father had said, as if giving him a word of warning, "but when she's taken as a whole, it'll become clear enough."

Shyrock dropped his hat back on his head and looked at August. "Though come ta think of it," he said, "I could use a visit by my granddaughters."

"We'll come over at six. I'll have Belle bring supper," August said without hesitation.

CHAPTER 16

POT CALLING THE KETTLE BLACK

As promised, August and his family showed up to Buck's at straight-up six o'clock. The girls ran in like storm troopers.

"Gwamps! Gwamps! Wah heah!" shouted Vivian. "Daddy said you missed us, but now wah heah, so you don't have to miss us anymowa!"

First, they fawned over Rebel, lying at Buck's feet, and then they turned their attention to their granddad, sitting by the kitchen table. Vivian jumped roughly on his lap and hugged him hard around the neck. Holly moved to his side, leaned forward, and kissed him on the cheek.

"Oh, have I ever missed you two little dandelions!" Buck hugged them both around the shoulders. He felt all the emptiness and dark shadows of the house retreat through the windows and the walls, no match for the two lively young girls.

Belle followed a few paces behind. "Hi, Dad," she said. "Hope you're not being mauled to death." She set a covered pan on the stove and crossed the kitchen to kiss him on the top of his head. "August told me you've had the kind of a day that is best forgotten."

"Yeah, forgetting it would be for the best. Thank you, Belle."

"Forget what, Mommy?" Holly asked.

"Gramps had a hard day is all."

"I'm sorry you had a bad day, Gramps," Holly said, leaning into him.

"Thanks, sweetheart," Buck said, reaching around her waist.

"Me, too!" Vivian gave him another squeeze around the neck.

"Vivian, a little more gentle, please," Belle admonished.

"Oh, I can take it," Buck said, laughing. "Helps keep me tough."

August came in last. "Well, Dad, here we are, as promised, the whole lot of us," he said.

"Yes, I can see that," Buck said, smiling happily. "The whole lot."

Buck tugged gently at Holly's thin waist. "I dusted off the ol' checker board, Lollipop. I feel lucky, so you better look out."

Lollipop. Buck thought of Ida and how delighted she would be right now, basking in the light of her granddaughters.

"I don't feel like playing checkers, Gramps. I'm sorry," Holly said. What happened at the grocery store was still pulling at her. It sapped her energy, especially now that her gramps was right next to her, reminding her of it. More than anything, she was worried he would see the change in her. What that change was, she wasn't sure.

"Lolli, not feelin' like playin' checkers!" Buck said, incredulous. "I won't believe it fer a second."

"Sorry, Gramps. I just don't." Holly looked forlorn, like she had disappointed him, and she felt awful about it. She lay her head on his shoulder.

"That's okay, sweetheart." Buck said, patting her on the arm, his voice gentle. "You don't have to apologize to your granddad." He exchanged looks with Belle. She raised her eyebrows. "No idea" was her unspoken message to him.

Belle hadn't told Buck about the girl's mysterious fatigue after returning home from the store. His worry whenever his granddaughters caught any little cold or bug was always way out of proportion with the actual illness. Belle and August figured it was from having lost Elizabeth, and they made adjustments in what they told him.

"I wiw pway checkahs wif you, Gwamps," Vivian chimed in.

"Okay, after supper. How 'bout that?" Buck told her.

"Okay," Vivian said happily, and jumped from his lap to do a little hoppy dance.

"You hungry, Dad?" Belle asked. "I brought over a beef roast like Mom used to make, with carrots and potatoes cooked on the side. Your favorite dish, if I'm not mistaken."

Buck nodded. "Every Sunday after you all came home from church." He had never gone to church, although he considered himself a religious man. His ferrying responsibilities accounted for part of it, but also, he believed that God was more present to him under the sky, in the great outdoors, than he ever would be under the roof of a church. Ida had read him reference after reference in the Bible that proved—in her mind and in the minds of many others, including the preacher, who had given a sermon on it—that the Lord wanted to be worshipped in a church built in his name. His temple. Shyrock didn't go for any of it.

"I reckon there's some mistake bein' made there. The Lord's temple don't have ta mean a building. God's creation, the out of doors, is a temple, and he meant it thatta way. It don't have ta mean you're right or I'm wrong—I only know what's fer me," he would say, dismissing the argument.

Finally, Ida had let him be. He believed in the Lord—that was the important thing, wasn't it? When she was in heaven, she hoped and she prayed that he would be there too.

After Ida died, Buck considered going to church to honor her, but he hadn't brought himself to do it yet. Who would he get to operate the ferry? August would still know how to run it, but Buck wouldn't think of asking him. He had made his feelings known well enough.

The girls set the table while Belle forked the roast, tender and falling off the bone, onto a platter. The good china platter had been Ida's, a wedding present. Belle stacked sliced bread on a plate and beside it placed a slab of butter.

≈ ≈ ≈

After supper, Buck and Vivian started their checkers game. The game mostly consisted of Buck finding a way to put his checkers in her path so she could jump him. Holly stood at Buck's elbow, watching the moves. "You're letting her win," she whispered in his ear.

Vivian heard her. Her eyes flashed. "He's not neitha wetting me win, Hawwy!" she shouted. On her knees, she twisted about in her chair.

Holly smiled in a knowing way.

Vivian went wild. Screaming, she slammed both of her little fists down on the checkerboard. The checker pieces bounced, willy-nilly, across the board.

"Whoa, Nellie!" Buck exclaimed, reaching over the table to try to calm her.

Vivian pushed his hands away and screamed louder. "He's not wetting me win!" She pounded on the checkerboard. "He's not! He's not wetting me win!"

Belle intervened. She rushed over to Vivian and squatted next to her chair. "Viv, it's okay. Don't listen to your sister." She gave Holly a dire look: *Keep your mouth shut.*

Holly didn't heed the warning. "She's just stubborn," she said.

"I'm *not stubbuhn*!" Vivian shrieked, her eyes filling with tears of rage. In her fit of anger, she lashed out at the first person who came into her field of vision—Buck, sitting directly across the table from her. "Gwamps is stubbuhn!" she yelled. "Daddy said so!"

Belle gathered her up, kicking and screaming, and carried her out of the room.

With the two of them gone, silence took command of the kitchen. Buck looked at the window straight in front of him, even though there was nothing to see but dark glass, reflecting his image back at him. He folded the checkerboard and laid it carefully in its box. Then, one by one, red pieces first, he pinched the checkers between his fingers and placed them in the box.

Holly looked at her father and then at her grandfather, waiting for one of them to say something. In another room, her mother was speaking firmly to Vivian. "That's enough now," she said. "Enough." Vivian had begun to cough, choking on her tears. Finally, her father stepped outside onto the porch.

"Next time I'll play checkers, I promise," Holly said to her grandpa, her voice wavering.

Buck turned to the girl and saw the look of shame, the feeling that she was somehow to blame. She was ready to cry. He wrapped his arm around her. "Listen, Lolli girl, it's not yer fault. It's grownup business. It has nothin' to do with you." He turned her chin so she was facing him. "Do you hear me?"

Holly looked at him and nodded her head. "Yes, I hear you, Gramps."

Oh, the depths of those eyes, he thought. *And so young still.* He saw something there he couldn't read.

Belle walked into the kitchen holding a contrite Vivian's hand. She looked confused, as if mystified by the force of her own outburst. "Where's August?" Belle asked. Her husband's disappearance and the somber look on Buck's face told her all she needed to know to answer her own question.

Buck pointed. "On the porch, I reckon."

As if on cue, a car horn blasted from below, rising up out of the wedge in the ground made by the ferry landing, as if it had been swallowed and needed help in extricating itself.

Buck was relieved, as much as he didn't want to admit it to himself. "Stick around if you want. I won't be long."

"No, we'll be going, I think," Belle said, knowing well enough when an evening was shot.

"Belle, I am thankful for your generosity. The pot roast was perfect."

"I had a good teacher."

"The best."

Belle smiled sadly and kissed Buck on the forehead. "Good night, Dad."

On his way out, Buck passed behind August, who stood at the porch rail gazing out over the river. Its ripples and swirls shone silver in the moonlight. Over to the left, on the Indiana side, a swath the width of five Main Streets had been scraped clean by a bulldozer. It glistened under the moon like a fresh, still-seeping wound.

"Pot callin' the kettle black," Buck said to his son's back as he passed. "And in fronta the girls ta boot."

"Well, shit," August muttered, after his father was beyond hearing range.

CHAPTER 17

DRESS SHOES

"I thought we had an agreement."

"What *agreement*?" August repeated the word back to his wife venomously. He was still off-kilter from the scene at his father's house, the whole "stubborn" business. He and Belle had walked back out to the truck after putting the girls to bed to carry out this discussion beyond their earshot. Belle had insisted on it, although August didn't see the need. They hadn't started the truck to run the heater for fear it would wake the girls. As a result, the windows of the truck had fogged over from the heat of their bodies and from the huffs of steam that plumed out of their mouths as if their insides had begun to boil.

"An understanding, then. That together we were going to help Dad, *your father*, through this hard time. Remember? He's losing his whole *way of life*."

"What is it I'm not doing, exactly?"

"Tonight, for example. Would it have killed you to say, 'I'm sorry, Dad. Sorry if I said you're stubborn'? He just pulled a dead man out of the river, for God's sake! Did you forget that?"

"It's not that simple."

"Not that simple." Belle shook her head but didn't give up. "Well, are you? Are you sorry?"

"Not sorry that I said it to you, no, because it's true. He's a stubborn old cuss, plain and simple. Am I sorry that it got back to him, especially through Vivian? Yes, that much I regret." August reached forward and wiped at the clouded windshield with the back of his hand. At his touch it turned to an icy scrim.

"So you could have said 'I'm sorry' then."

August looked where the spot on the windshield that he'd touched had begun repairing itself, fogging back over. "What difference would that have made, Belle? Tell me. Tell me right now, what difference would it have made?"

"You've got to start somewhere." Belle wished they could both stop breathing long enough so the windows wouldn't fog over so bad. It felt to her like there wasn't room enough inside the truck for her and all the puffed up self-righteousness that was her husband.

"Oh, brother," August said, rolling his eyes. "You are somethin', you know that? You're too innocent is what you are. It's because you don't have the first idea what it's like."

"Oh!" Belle floundered in the dark with her hand, trying to find the door handle. "Oh!"

August reached to grab the sleeve of her coat just as her fingers wrapped around the lever. "Get your hands off me!" she screamed, swatting at him as the door flew open.

"Belle, get back in here!"

"You! You coldhearted . . . animal!" Belle leaned forward, bent at the waist, her hair hanging loose in front of her shoulders. She fired the words at him through the open door she'd just flung aside. "I can't *believe* you would use that against me!"

August bent sideways toward her under the harsh dome light, still reaching with his arm. "I'm sorry!"

"Oh! He *can* say it!" she shouted. "The great man has spoken the oh-so-impossible words! Well, I am so sick of you and your selfish, stupid pride!"

"Belle, you're gonna wake up the girls. Get back in the truck so we can iron this out."

"Go to hell!" she screamed. "I'm not ironing anything out with you! I hope you stay in there and freeze to death!" She turned and marched toward the house. The yellow trail of light spilling down the length of the sidewalk lit her way, as if sympathetic to her cause. Once inside, she latched the door and flipped the lock.

"Did I wake you, sweetheart?" Belle hurried to where Holly stood sleepily in the doorway between the kitchen and living room. She laid her hand on Holly's head and turned her gently toward the girls' bedroom. "C'mon, I'll tuck you back in bed."

"Why were you yelling, Mommy?"

"You heard me yelling? Well, yes," Belle said, surrendering, "I suppose you did." She tucked the covers snugly around Holly and sat next to her bed, running her fingers through the girl's hair, being careful not to pull at it when her fingertips became entangled in the thick curls.

"Why, Mommy? Were you and Daddy fighting?"

"Yes, honey, we were fighting."

"Why?" Holly's voice sounded small and vulnerable in the huge gaping darkness.

Belle tried to think how to answer this question without causing her daughter to worry. She refused to lie to her, but she didn't want to provide her with more information than she needed to know. "Well, your father and I sometimes see things differently. And when your dad makes a mistake, it's very hard for him to admit it."

"Is this about Daddy calling Gramps stubborn?"

"Yes, it is. I want your dad to apologize, but he won't do it."

"Why not?" Holly's eyes were beginning to droop. When she was just about to drop off to sleep, they flew open again.

"I don't know. It's just hard for him, I guess."

"Should I ask him to?"

"No, no, you stay out of it. Your dad will have to figure it out for himself."

"Will he, do you think?

"I'm sure he will. Here, lift your head." Belle plumped up Holly's pillow and when she had settled into it again, she told her to go back to sleep. She kissed her on the cheek.

"No, I mean, will he freeze to death?"

"No, Daddy won't freeze to death. He knows how to take care of himself."

"I love you, Mommy," Holly said.

"I love you, too, Lollipop."

"And I love Daddy, too."

"Of course you do."

Back in her own room, Belle thought of her words to her daughter. *I'm sure he will.* Did she mean it, or was it just wishful thinking? Truth be told, she wasn't sure of anything lately, and that wasn't like her. This new crisis in their family had brought out a side of August she had never seen before—a side she didn't like at all. For him to bring up her own family's tragedy in such a callous way was something she never would have expected from him.

When she was eight, almost as old as Holly was now, her mother and father had been killed in a car crash on the way home from church one night. The country road was a series of small, knobby hills, one after the other. The narrow road dipped down into sudden hollows and just as quickly rose up the other side to the crest of the next hill. At the top of one of these, they met a car, going too fast and traveling in the middle of the road. Her mother and father were killed instantly, as were the people in the other vehicle. Belle was asleep in the backseat and woke up on the floorboard, covered with glass. Afterward, she had no memory of the crash.

There was a picture in the newspaper of her little white dress shoes, covered with grime and filth, lying on their sides close to one another in the ditch. Her grandmother cut it out and showed it to her much later, after she'd turned eighteen. Belle cried in her bed the whole afternoon. But that evening, she sat down to supper feeling lighter, as if an unnamed burden that had been pressing on her chest like a stone throughout most of her childhood and adolescence had finally been lifted from her.

After the crash, Belle was raised by her grandparents. In her own words to August, "They spoiled me rotten. Gave me everything I wanted. Trying to make up for me losing my mom and dad, I suppose." And because of this, he said she didn't have the first idea of what it was like to have Dad as a father.

It was beginning to feel like August was no longer the man she had married, or maybe she hadn't really known him all along.

CHAPTER 18

CROSSING FROM ONE SIDE TO THE OTHER

Locked out of the house, August ran through his options. There weren't many. He couldn't pound on the door, demanding to be let in, as that would scare the girls. They had probably woken them up with their yelling. He could go to his old man's house—he wouldn't ask questions, but there would be some untold price to pay down the road. He couldn't go to Abel's Hotel. It would be all over town before dinnertime the next day.

One thing for sure, he couldn't stay in the truck. As Belle had pointed out, he would probably freeze to death before morning. Drifting south of town on the river road, he thought of Virgil.

Virgil lived out at Cheetham's Camp, a muddle of ratty fishing shacks and old, broken-down school buses with the wheels, fenders, and hoods all wrenched loose and hauled off; their motors, too, were long gone. The camp looked out over the river from a tall bank southeast of town. Virgil's bus hunkered into the ground at one end of the camp, next to where the woods started. He was the camp's only full-time resident; most people came out only on weekends. Virgil, August knew, wasn't one to gossip.

August knocked on the makeshift door, rattling it on its hinges. A curtain on one of the many windows running all along the side of Virgil's "cabin" was brushed aside. Then August could hear him shuffling down the length of the old bus, cursing when he stumbled against something in the dark. When the door finally opened, Virgil stood there in his pajamas, looking like he'd just crawled off his deathbed. His thick white hair was disheveled, and in the harsh glare of the outside light, his eyes were dark hollows in a deeply creviced face. He squinted and ran a hand over his face, as if he might be seeing something that wasn't there. "August?" he marveled, and waved him in.

Virgil's kitchen was just big enough for a small square table to be crowded against the outside wall. He pulled out one of the chairs and told August to sit. Stoop-shouldered, he shuffled his slippered feet across the chilly linoleum floor, the colors of which were worn to nothing along its most frequented paths. He lit the tiny gas stove with a match and then poured ground coffee into the bottom of a metal pot. After splashing in some water, he set it on top of the burner. "You look cold, m'boy. Coffee won't take long."

Virgil lowered himself slowly into the other chair, ran both hands backward over his mess of hair, and looked at August, waiting for him to say something. When he didn't, Virgil asked, "What's the occasion? Not that I hafta know."

"Disturbing your sleep, I suppose you have the right."

"If havin' my sleep disturbed gave me special rights, I reckon I'd be the Duke of Earl by now." Virgil reached for his tobacco and rolling papers and stifled a yawn.

"Belle locked me out. Until she cools down, I best not go back."

"Oh, the wrath of a woman," Virgil said and shook his head knowingly. "I don't know what ta tell ya, m'boy. You're talkin' to an old man who's wore out two wives and is sorry, too late, for all of it. Drinkin', ya know. My word on the subject wouldn't be worth a hill o' beans."

In spite of himself, August chuckled. "You're too hard on yourself, Virgil," he said.

"Doubt that's true," Virgil answered. "Maybe not hard enough."

"Well, anyway, it's the same thing we talked about before—the old man and what I'm doin' or not doin' to help him with the bridge."

"Hmmm, the old man again." Virgil scratched his head and smoothed back his hair again, but it sprang back up defiantly. "How's he doin'?"

"I dunno." August shrugged. "He barely talks to me. Bad blood, I reckon you'd call it. The whole ferry thing. Family tradition and all."

"That ship's done sailed. Ain't your fault he can't accept it."

"Yeah, well, like I told you before, Virgil, Belle don't see it that way. I'm supposed to coddle and nurse him along through this 'end of an era' thing, or whatever it's called." August looked at the ceiling, studying a dirty cobweb in the corner that hung like a loosely slung hammock. Virgil's cabin was cold and damp, so August kept his coat on. "As far as I can see," he continued, "the age of the ferry's been endin' for a long time. Good thing I stayed away from it."

"That's right. Happenin' all over. Millerville's one o' the last, on the Wabash leastways. I haven't said it 'til now, and I'm still sorry to say it, but your daddy's had his head stuck in the sand." Virgil stood up and shuffled over to the stove to check on the coffee. When he reached to pull cups and saucers from a shelf, his pajama bottoms rose up enough to reveal spindly, hairless ankles and dry, cracked skin, sectioned off roughly into rows and columns as if drawn there by a pencil guided by an unsteady hand.

Seeing the old man's frailness, August felt sudden remorse for waking him and then pestering him with his own problems. "Virgil, let's forget about the coffee. You go back to bed, and I'll find a spot to lay my head, if you don't mind."

"It's 'bout ready."

August could tell the old man's heart wasn't in it, that he'd much rather be back in his warm bed. "Nah, sorry I didn't say somethin' sooner. Let's forget about it. It'll just keep me awake anyhow."

"Well, I'll get ya a piller and a couple blankets then," Virgil said. "You can bed down on the davenport."

"That would be fine," August said.

Virgil handed August the bedclothes, assuring him that things would look brighter in the morning. "Always do," Virgil said and added with a cackle, "unless you got a hangover."

"Thanks, Virgil."

"It's okay. I can't remember the last time I had an overnight guest, favorable or otherwise." He stood there a moment, teetering slightly, as if trying to recall the last time someone had stayed the night. Then he shook his head, apparently having failed. "Hope you're warm enough."

"Better than sleepin' in a truck," August said, folding a scratchy wool blanket into halves before laying it on Virgil's musty-smelling sofa.

"Reckon that much is true," Virgil agreed, disappearing into the dark.

August pulled off his boots and coat and covered himself with the other blanket. He would go home first thing in the morning, before the girls were up, and promise Belle he'd try harder. What that might entail, he wasn't sure, but the least he could do was try. He shouldn't have brought up that thing about her family. It wasn't right. He thought then of his old man and saw the mulish set of his jaw. Anger percolated up from the base of his chest. "Impossible," he said quietly, out of some inner need to assert himself against the shame of being locked out of his own house. "Goddamn impossible."

Buck lay awake that night thinking about the drowned man—the gray, bloated, stinking nightmare of a thing he'd dragged out of the river. How had the man ended up there, face down in the river? Was it an accident? Had he fallen in? Or had he jumped? If so, what drove men to such drastic and deadly measures? Buck tried to picture it—the force behind such desperation. Whatever it was, Buck couldn't summon it into the clearness of thought. It was too dark—dark and horrible and mean.

After Ida died, he had felt that thing. It had climbed on his shoulder, clung to his neck, and pressed on his jugular with its sharp claws. It breathed in his ear, and its raspy, hollow breath sucked him dry and left him empty—empty as the riverbed depleted of its water, its lifeblood gone.

But ultimately, during his waking hours, the ferry and the river were what saved him—something as simple as crossing from one side to the other, the repetition and routine of it, the scratch of the ferry's apron in the sand on the Indiana shore, and the bump and scrape of the cement landing on the Illinois bank. And all the while, the Wabash followed its own purposes, always flowing, its course set. It kept a rhythm by which he could time his life.

In this way, the insistent, the unthinkable, was held at bay.

Just before he drifted off to sleep, lulled by his thoughts of riding the river, another image tried pushing its way into his mind. But he was too far gone into the mercy of slumber for it to coalesce into anything beyond a single strand of wire arcing through the misted air, about to connect one bank to the other.

CHAPTER 19

PECKING AT THE SAME KERNEL OF CORN

After the flood subsided, the old fellas returned, as devoted to the bridge construction project as those being paid cash money to build it. Nothing could shoo them away—not the stench of mud and mucky sand, not the choke of diesel fumes. As the workers carved out the hole inside the cofferdam frame with a clam bucket, the retirees stood with their arms crossed, at a distance tolerable to all, and took it all in. They nodded assent or, if called for, shook their heads doubtfully at each new turn of events.

When excavation moved to the east main pier foundation, the old men wanted a closer look. There were seven of them on foot, who stepped sideways, slowly and gingerly, down the steep ferry landing. As if going for a picnic and a ball game afterward, they were in a jubilant mood, chattering and laughing the whole way down.

While crossing on the ferry, they were puzzled when Buck showed no interest in joining their fun. The loudest of the bunch, Chester Howe, was a bald, corpulent man with Coke-bottle glasses. He had been a welder by trade. The glasses gave his eyes an over-magnified look, making Buck want to take a step back when he approached. His legs were short in proportion to his body and looked to have been sawed off at the knees. Retirement suited him better than work ever had. When it came to standing around and playing the fool and rolling his big eyes around in their exaggerated sockets, there was no match for Chester Howe. He put on his best limp and approached Shyrock at his station in the steer boat.

"Buck, you shoulda sawr it. The diver, I'm tellin' ya. Dropped natural as a tadpole inta that hole they dug out." Chester imitated the diver's motion with his hand and at the same time dropped his huge eyeballs in their sockets. "Like he was born to it, I'm tellin' ya. Made it look so easy, me and the boys almost followed him in. It was somethin', I'm tellin' ya. Rilly somethin'."

"He can't hear you," Jaybird Grant, another of the retired men, shouted over the thump of the motor.

Buck looked downriver. He could hear him fine. But there was nothing more infuriating, to his mind, than a bunch of idle old men standing around like hens pecking at the same kernel of corn. "If I ever come to that, Lord, drown me," he muttered under his breath.

Someone else yelled out to Chester and pointed excitedly upriver. The claw bucket on the Indiana side had taken its first gulp of sand. Chester hightailed it across the deck to rejoin his group as fast as his stubby legs would carry him.

Their lively chatter continued all the way across the river, as if real decisions were being made and obvious mistakes put to rights. Buck couldn't wait to get them off his ferry. If he had his way, they could swim back to Millerville.

LOG ENTRY: 28 February, 1939. Since my last entry, steel-sheet piles were set up around the inside of the cofferdam frame and driven a short distance.

Additional framing was added and driven down as the excavation progressed. The steel sheeting was driven ahead of the excavation, holding a minimum toe-in of about 5 feet. When firm shale was encountered at an elevation of 2 feet above the proposed bottom of the foundation, it was broken up by dropping a pointed, 60-foot section of railroad rail into it and was removed by a clam bucket on the derrick.

After most of the material was removed by this method, a diver was employed to complete the excavation. Working in 30 feet of water, this diver used a jackhammer to loosen and level the material in the bottom of the foundation. Most of his work was around the edge of the cofferdam and under the framing, where the pointed rail could not be used. After loosening the material, he pulled it to the center of the hole where it could be removed by the clam bucket. A very satisfactory base for the foundation was secured in this manner.

Because the cofferdam is not to be unwatered until after the footing has been poured, I inspected this foundation by sounding over the area with a steel rod and making visual inspection of the last material removed from the hole.

CHAPTER 20

SOME KINDA DOG

Will Turner and his drinking associate, Eddie Simms, pulled up to the Indiana ferry landing. Eddie was driving, but Turner reached over and laid on the horn. Eddie shoved his hand away. "I can blow my own goddamned horn," he said.

"I'm fuggin' jealous," Turner said, laughing at his own cleverness. Turner was flushed crimson from a night of heavy drinking. Liquor made him meaner than he already was.

"Screw you," Eddie said. Eddie, unlike the muscular Turner, was a runt. He appeared malnourished, as if his growth had been impeded early on. Maybe his old granddad had been right: "Boy, you eatin' too much watermelon. Too much watermelon stunt your growth." Eddie did love fresh watermelon. He ate it all summer and into the fall, as long as watermelon was in season, seeds and all. His own heavy drinking plus three packs of smokes a day probably didn't help either.

Turner went for the horn again. Eddie Simms punched his forearm.

"Ya scrawny li'l bastard," Turner growled, rubbing his arm. "I oughta smazh yer face in."

"I warned ya."

Turner glared at him, his eyes damp and bleary, but he didn't reach for the horn again. He tried to focus on the opposite side of the river. It was early morning, before light, and even sober he wouldn't have been able to see that far in the dark. "I'm fuggin' sig o' waitin' for tha' old bastard. Where da hell is he?"

"Give 'im a break. Poor ol' guy never gets a full night's sleep."

"Fugg him and the horze . . ." Turner belched. "Horze he rode in on."

"You're a genius. Anybody ever tell you that before?"

"Ma dear ol' mom, 'til I proved I wasn't." He cackled belligerently and then started rolling down his window. His arm jerked unevenly, having trouble following the circular path of the window crank. When his hand slipped off the crank, he yelled, "Fugg it!" He rammed his arm through the half-opened window and dropped the beer can he'd just drained off. Then he bellowed out the window. "You fuggin' ol' cunt, git your zarry, wrinkled azz over here!"

Simms shook his head. While he lit a cigarette, Turner gave the horn a quick blast.

"That's the last time, Turner. I'm sick o' yer ugly face. I don't need yer shit." Simms threw his Zippo on the dash, and it bounced up and hit the windshield, hard.

"Breag yer own goddamn winzhield," Turner said, rolling his eyes. "Dumb-azz."

"Good luck findin' yerself another drinkin' buddy," Simms grumbled.

"You made tha' promizz afore, azzhole."

The low thump of a motor started up across the way. After a few moments more, it rose slightly in pitch, getting purchase on air and gas and shaking off the damp.

"There he is. Pretty fast work in my book," Simms said.

A single light flashed on at water level. The night was clear with a cold breeze frisking its way downriver from the north. The white beam illuminated the flow and punch of the main channel, revealing, as if seen from a great distance, vast, misty peaks and steep, craggy valleys shifting and reshaping themselves, as if time itself was fluid.

"Fasz, ma azz. When the bridge is billed, we woan' way' atall." Turner dug around in his shirt pocket for a cigarette. "I'd be home a'ready, zleepin' like a fuggin' baby." When he finally managed to retrieve a smoke, the fire from his lighter seemed to dodge its tip, like a game of cat-and-mouse, and only through stubborn persistence did he get finally get it lit. Since guzzling that last beer, Turner's slurring had grown steadily worse. The car lights were off, but in the glow of cigarettes Eddie saw his head wander from side-to-side.

Seeing two lights from the ferry instead of one, Turner closed one eye. Sloppily, he flung his arm across the car. His elbow hit Simms, and he almost spilled sideways in the seat as he slapped his hand onto the horn ring again, holding it there.

"Christ! He's comin', okay? Can you get that through your thick skull?"

"Parteee!" Turner bellowed. This was Turner's mantra, Simms had learned, when in his final stages of intoxication, before he fell and butchered himself or simply passed out. It was hard to tell which would come first.

The light beam grew slowly in size, and the motor beat louder until the outline of the ferry's bow came dimly into view below the headlamp, which was mounted just above Shyrock's head. Shyrock cut the throttle and let the ferry glide into the sandbank.

Once landed, Shyrock went through his usual routine. Finished, he stood at the front of the ferry and shouted, "Switch on your headlamps, and I'll turn off this 'un so's you can see where you're headed."

A low, barely audible growl came from the back of Turner's throat. He glared at the ferry operator through the windshield.

"Better behave yourself, Will," Simms warned.

"Mind y'own fuggin' bizness," Turner slurred, his eyes locked on Shyrock. "Ol' sump pu' me in jail."

As soon as they pulled onto the ferry, Buck stepped up to Simms's window. He sized up the situation quickly. The smell of liquor was enough to turn his stomach. Will Turner was in the car, leering at him, his face lit green from the panel light. Buck told Simms to leave the car in low gear. And then he said, "You boys must be partial ta the sound o' that horn."

Turner rammed his door open with his shoulder and stumbled out of the car. Simms thought for sure he would go right on over the side of the ferry, but he managed, somehow, to keep a hold on the door. Turner looked over the roof of the car, the same leering, sloppy expression on his face. "'At wuz me blowin' tha' horn, ol' man. Doan' like it?" Turner swayed precariously.

Simms climbed out of the car and started around the front to get Turner back in the car before he fell over the side.

"Sorry, Mr. Shyrock. Afraid we've both had a few beers."

"I carry those who's drunk same as those who's sober."

"Ya callin' me a drunk?" Turner said, trying to push past Simms.

"Ain't callin' nobody a drunk." Buck wasn't easily ruffled. This was nothing new to him. He'd seen many a man come back from driving the bottoms with empty bottles clanking around on the floorboard. Turner had been on his ferryboat drunk on several occasions but not since the gas-stealing incident that had landed him in jail. He was always surly but never this bad. *A mean drunk, this one*, Buck thought. *Like his old man.*

Buck got the ferry moving. Turner had worked himself around to the front of the car, pushing past Simms. As Buck accelerated, Turner toppled onto the hood of the car and grabbed hold of the hood ornament.

"Did it on purpose, ya ol' fugg!" Turner yelled over the top of the motor noise.

Buck kept looking ahead, ignoring him.

Simms stepped in front of Turner again, trying to block his path to Shyrock, but Turner mowed right over the smaller man, knocking him to the deck. "Ya thing ya kin 'nore me!" he roared, stumbling toward the steer boat. "See 'at 'ere!" he yelled, pointing unsteadily in the general direction of the west main pier construction site, either not seeing or not caring that it was totally dark not much farther out than the end of his finger. "Gonna put ya right outta a job, ol' man," he said, jabbing his finger. "Ya outta a job!"

When Turner was almost to the steer boat, Rebel leaped up out of it, snarling. Her teeth flashing, she hit Turner in midair, hard in the center of the chest. Turner stumbled backward and fell onto his back. Rebel stood firm, head down, blocking his path to Shyrock. Her hackles stood out on her back like knives. Her glare fixed on Turner, the hound continued to growl—her long, sharp teeth on display, her lips flared and frothing. She showed she meant every kind of business. Sprawled out and moaning on the deck, Turner twisted his head from side to side as if trying to work out in his addled mind how he had ended up where he was.

Eddie Simms stood and brushed himself off, saying, "That's some kinda dog, Mr. Shyrock."

"Yep, some kinda dog," Buck agreed. He whistled to the hound, and she jumped back into the boat, her hackles settling slowly into her back.

"Sorry, Mr. Shyrock, for the trouble."

Buck nodded his head. "Better find yourself another sidekick, son," he said. "This one behaves bad."

Once they bumped against shore, Turner pulled himself up by the car's bumper to a sitting position. He looked around for the dog. Not seeing it, he struggled to his feet. He stumbled around to the open passenger door, but before dropping into the car, he glared at Buck. "You an' tha' dog in trouble," he said, plain as day, as if the hard fall had cleared his head. "Real bad trouble."

"Git off my ferry," Buck said, meeting his eye.

CHAPTER 21

LET THERE BE LIGHT!

Belle hesitated on the porch a few moments and gaped at the changes across the river. A large swath of trees had been cleared on the Indiana bank, and from the river back to the levee, the ground was ripped apart from the excavation. Men and their equipment worked around several large holes, surrounded by piles of wet sand and mud. The noise was nearly constant. The colossal pounding of steel on steel echoed from one bank to the other and back again, until it was hard to tell which was the initial strike and which the reverberation. The roar of diesel engines and the foul, throat-clogging odor of diesel fuel drifted over the river in black clouds as men tried to shout over it all.

It was a different place now. Belle couldn't begin to imagine how this must make Dad feel, being here day in and day out, no escaping it.

It was just before noon. Belle carried a wicker basket with a canning jar of green beans from last year's garden and a goulash made with ground chuck, still warm from the oven. She turned and opened the front door and called into the house. "Dad," she said, "I brought you your dinner."

She heard the dog first, panting, and then its nails scratching on the wooden porch steps behind her, followed a second later by Buck's voice. "Here we are," he said.

Rebel pranced up to sniff the food. Belle patted her on the side of her neck. "Not for you. Sorry."

Buck chuckled. "Somethin' fer me then, I reckon."

"Yes, not much, but it's something. Still early for the garden. The beans need to be cooked a bit."

He lifted the cloth and peeked over the edge of the basket. "Mmm, smells good. Come on in. You'll hafta join me."

Belle had not seen him for well over a week. In the light of day, he looked tired. His face sagged, and Belle could see he had lost more weight. His denim shirt hung loosely on his shoulders in a way it never had before. His eyes had lost more of their sparkle, like a light dimming in degrees. Belle wanted to cry, but she kept her face straight and focused on breathing normally.

Once they were inside the house, Buck asked, "How'd ya git here?"

"Oh, I walked. Fresh air did me good. Spring's in the air," she said, smiling, making a show of lightheartedness.

Buck's eyes flickered a moment at the thought of his daughter-in-law walking through the village with a wicker basket under her arm, delivering dinner to his house. "Where's Lolli and Viv?"

"Holly's in school, and Vivian's playing with a neighbor girl."

"Lol's in school, sure," he nodded. "I hope Viv's behavin' herself at that other girl's house. That little pipsqueak sure has a wild streak."

Belle set the basket on the table. "Oh, yes," she said, "doesn't she now? I'm still sorry about her behavior the last time we were all here."

Buck shrugged his shoulders, dismissing her concern. "Nah, nah, I'm the one should be sorry," he said. "I shoulda stayed plumb out of it. I just made it worse."

He looked around the kitchen. "This place needs a pickin' up. I wasn't expectin' ya."

Except for a dirty pan on the stove and a few dishes beside the wash pan, it looked the same as always—dusky; little sign of life. Like its occupants had moved out without taking any of their possessions. A thin cottoning of dust lay over everything. Belle resisted the urge to throw open the shades; to begin pounding seat cushions and shaking out rugs; to sweep, sweep, sweep, dust, dust, dust. She reminded herself it was not her house. She needed to be careful not to intrude, not to offend him.

"I didn't light the cookstove this mornin', but I'll stoke it up for ya enough for the beans." Buck reached for kindling in a square wooden box next to the stove.

"Yes, a nice fire will do the trick," Belle said.

He creaked open the side door on the massive old stove that he always kept blacked to perfection, even now, and with a series of quick snaps broke up some small, dry twigs and placed them in a neat pile inside the stove's belly. He lit a wooden match on the side of the stove and held it to the bottom of the sticks. As the twigs began crackling, he slowly added kindling. A wisp of smoke escaped out the stove door and then, shortly, Buck shoved in a couple of larger pieces of wood and closed the door. Before long, the heat of the fire was yowling up the stovepipe.

Belle looked around the kitchen. "Dad, how about now you got the stove lit, you sit down and rest. I'll get the kitchen looking spic-and-span while we wait for the beans to cook."

"Nah. Nah. You don't need to come over here and clean up my mess. I won't have it."

"You know better than to try and stop a woman when she's set her mind to something," Belle said, trying her best to make it a joke.

"Yeah, I was married to one of the most stubborn women on earth, I do believe, so I know. But I still don't like you havin' to do my cleanin'." After a moment of looking around the room, Buck shook his head. "I do reckon Ida would have my tail feathers for lettin' the place go like this."

That put it to rest. His resolve had weakened. Belle could tell by the sound of his voice that he didn't like it, but he wouldn't try to stop her. "Better make that fire a little bigger so I can heat a pot of water for cleaning," she said.

Belle found one of Ida's old aprons, a faded flower print with turquoise stamens in the middle of curving yellow petals, worn to a pleasing softness from its many washings. Ida had loved flowers. It lay in a drawer with her other aprons in the wash basin cabinet. Belle found it touching that Buck hadn't disturbed them. The crisp folds in the apron were put there by Ida herself. Belle wondered if Buck ever opened the drawer to have a look. She almost felt guilty disturbing this one from its resting place. She would place it at the bottom of the stack after she had laundered it, so Ida's touch would still be on those most visible.

Buck stared at her as she wrapped it around her hips and knotted the tie at the back of her waist. The look on his face was one of melancholy, but of gladness, too, that she had put it on, as if she was doing it for him, to help him remember a happier time. He kept quiet, finally looking away.

Belle dug around the open shelves on the wall opposite the stove until she found a pot to heat the cleaning water. She filled it from the pump and carried it to the stove. Next, she poured beans into a pan and set them on the warming stove.

Belle felt the bottom of the casserole dish. Good—still warm enough to eat.

Once she'd served him, Buck spoke around his food. "August. How's he?"

"Same. Busy. Time of year, I suppose."

"Mind if I give a little to the dog?" he asked.

"Not from the table!" she scolded, as if he were a child. "Here, I'll do it." She spooned some goulash from the casserole dish into Rebel's pan over by the counter. The dog went to work.

"Busy," Buck said, hesitating in his eating. "We're all busy. How is it that we're all so busy all the time?"

Belle looked at his broad back, bent over the table. He wasn't usually the pensive type, at least not outwardly. "Well, I don't know. We just are, I suppose."

"Umm," he grunted.

"You, for example," Belle said. "You're always busy, always on the move. Matter of fact, I don't know how you've kept ahead of it all for so long. The river, the work, the people. Always on duty. It'd wear most men to a frazzle." She was careful not to say, "You deserve retirement."

"Yeah, but there's times I can sit with my boots off, roughin' my dog, talkin' nonsense at her."

"Uh-huh," she said, letting him talk. She moved to the stove. The cleaning water was just beginning to steam. It curled up out of the pan in an intricate, weaving dance.

The sight of it cheered Belle. *"A watched pot never boils."* Just a saying, but she knew it to be untrue. She had watched many a pot come to a boil. Always, she saw steam rising from a pan as a symbol of possibility, of great promise. Rising with that steam, from that small start, came the first steps that ripened into a life lived with hot, nourishing food, boosting it onward to bigger, grander designs. *Where would we be without it?* Belle liked to think of it in terms of all the kitchens in the world, the same thing repeated every time a pot started to boil, clear back through time. *Dreamy, and silly, probably, but oh well.*

"And I don't see it that way," Buck added, "the river wearin' me to a frazzle."

I didn't say that, exactly—the river, she thought. *Funny how he went there.*

Just then a dreadful pounding started from up at the bridge site. Ripples appeared in the water on the stove, a bouncing dot in the middle expanding out in circles to the edges of the kettle. Belle could feel the vibration in her feet.

Buck hesitated but appeared otherwise oblivious to the noise, although she knew he wasn't—that it was only a show for her benefit. Between the poundings, Belle could hear his breath as it entered and left his nose—a small, barely audible whistle accompanied each departing breath.

"Nah, I don't see it that way atall," he said. "I see it as the river puttin' up with me and all my shenanigans. My fits and moods is the way Ida used to say it. The river would be just fine without us all, Belle. And someday it will."

He stopped and pondered it a moment. *And someday it will.* The river, he believed, was eternal, while the rest of it, the rest of *them* . . . "I reckon what I'm really tryin' to say is . . ."

He waited, trying to get the words right. "Ferryin' ain't like it used ta be," he said, finally.

"What do you mean?"

"Hard sayin' exactly."

"Try," she said kindly. *Keep talking*, she said to herself, carrying the heavy, steaming pot back over to the counter, the one he'd built himself out of rough lumber and painted a pale, weedy green. Not pretty to the eye, but functional—poor Ida, living with this man and his backward ways all those years.

"I'm talkin' even before that." He jerked his head in the direction of the heavy pounding—*kaWHOMPa!*—repeating every few seconds—*kaWHOMPa!*—resounding and steady as the thumping of a heart. "Used ta be a ferry was a village thing—ya know, everyone pitchin' in some little way. People didn't even ask. They just did it, like it was theirs. Whether it be nailin' a loose board back tight to the railin' or sometimes even sweepin' the deck."

Buck started to laugh. His eyebrows, thick and bushy, gone wild since Ida wasn't there to pluck them, arched upward. "I remember one time ol' Gladdy Booker pullin' a broom out o' the back o' her husband Jess's truck. 'Stephen Shyrock,' she grumbled at me, 'how d'you put up with yourself?'" Buck, still shaking with laughter, shook his head at the memory of it. "She swept the whole dang deck, her broom and the dust just a-flyin' in the time it took us to cross over to Indiana. Musta looked from the bank like the ferry'd been lit afire."

Laughing with him, Belle asked, "And now—how is it now?"

"Now? People don't even think 'bout the ferry anymore, unless they have to cross. It's just a means, more'n a way o' life like it used ta be." Looking at his food, he shook his head. "I can do it m'self. During the flood, I even winched it out and back in by m'self. But still, it's diff'rent."

"Dad, you never ask for help!" Belle admonished. "If you'd ask, I'm sure people would help you. August and I would've helped you." Belle dipped some of the hot water into the wash basin and added soap.

"August has weighed in on that one, I'm afraid. Besides, he's got his own work to do."

Belle avoided the topic of August and his not following his father onto the ferry. No winning that one. She retrieved Buck's dishes from the table and dropped his plate into the dishwater. She watched as it sank, pendulum-like, to the bottom.

"It's changed, Belle. It's not the same, that's for certain. I never had ta ask. Ferryin' just ain't the same. No way."

They grew quiet. The only sound was his breathing through his nose. The drumming up at the construction site had stopped.

He started to tell her, almost saying, *Ya know what my real problem is, Belle?* But he stopped himself. That would be taking it too far, saying it. *I can't hear the river no more. It don't speak ta me like it used ta do. Not since the bridge started. I can't hear it no matter how hard I try.* She'd think he'd gone plumb crazy. Dropped over the edge. *Belle, you mightn't believe this, but the river has somethin' to say. Somethin' real important. We just hafta listen, is all.* No, as much as he needed to say it to someone, he couldn't. He didn't dare.

"What about that little girl?" he said instead.

"Which little girl?"

"Lolli."

"What do you mean?"

"She's worried 'bout me."

"No more than she worries about any of us. I think she's a natural-born worrier, like her Grandma Ida," she said, trying to put him off.

"She's worried 'bout me, Belle. I saw it in her face that time y'all brought over dinner. You remember."

Like her grandma, my eye, Belle thought. *She's like him, through and through—seeing, knowing, before things happen sometimes. Making herself sick.* Thank Jesus, August and Vivian hadn't inherited that trait. She didn't know if she could stand another one.

"We all are, Dad. Truth be told. We all are."

He harrumphed and shrugged his big shoulders in an uncharacteristic, loose-jointed kind of way, not liking that she had dodged his question. "What is there to worry about? I always take care o' m'self," he grumbled.

Oh my, Belle thought, *back to his old stubborn self.* Just like that, he had put his guard up, wishing he hadn't said so much, most likely. Probably because she had put hers up, no matter how momentarily and no matter how hard she tried to hide it. August was silk in comparison. After their fight, he had promised to try to be more understanding of his father. Said he knew why it needed to be done (although he wasn't very convincing when he said this). He'd even apologized to her.

Buck suddenly remembered. "You didn't eat," he said.

"Not hungry," she said, feeling peevish. This was all so hard. Did Millerville really have to have a bridge? Couldn't things just stay the way they were?

A horn bleated down on the landing. Buck's whole manner changed, his attention shifting away from her. "Here I go," he said. He reached for his hat and boots, pulled them on, and rose from the table. "Come on, Rebel, we got work ta do."

The dog had been asleep on the floor between Buck and the stove, but she quickly jumped up, looking groggy in the face as if trying to remember where she was. But then, in an instant, she was ready to go, wagging her tail and licking Buck on the hand.

Belle walked them to the door. Before leaving, he kissed her on the top of the head, a rare—in fact, extremely rare—show of physical affection and tenderness toward her. "Thanks, Belle."

"Bye, Dad. I'll keep cleaning up."

"I won't try and stop ya, since you'll do it anyhow."

After he left, Belle dropped onto a chair and looked around the kitchen. She had failed him. How exactly, she couldn't think, but her failure glared back at her, from the dull sheen of the pot she had plopped back on the stove to heat more water for cleaning to the yellowing, cracked window shades. The gray, pitiless half-light of the room mocked her and her penny-ante effort. The coating of dust on everything rebuked her. The heat from the stove was, all at once, suffocating.

She leaped up and rushed around the house, flinging open all the window shades, raising windows as far up as the frames would allow. Nothing and no one would mock her or her family. Light! Light! Let there be light!

CHAPTER 22

THE SEAGULL

The following morning, early, Buck spotted a white seagull, wings tipped in black, like they'd been dipped in ink, heading downriver. It flew just above tree level, straight and steady, not looking to either side. He watched until it disappeared around the bend. Rebel, too, fixed her gaze on it until it was gone. Never had Shyrock seen a seagull, except in pictures. He hadn't heard of anyone else seeing one either. *Leastways, not in these parts.*

"That was a seagull, by God," he said to the hound. "You ever see a seagull?" He pulled off his hat and scratched his bare crown. "I'll be damned."

Once he got over the surprise of it, Buck took it as a sign. Like he'd almost told Belle, the river hadn't spoken to him since that morning the man stood on the Indiana bank, holding his papers. He'd waited and waited and listened, his ear always cocked a little to the side, but nothing. Now this. A seagull. On the Wabash. The world as he knew it was in an awful flux, about to change to something he could not even imagine.

He had better get a grip on himself.

LOG ENTRY: 15 March, 1939. I have fallen behind in my logging, so I expect this entry will be a long one. It is night, and a gentle rain falls outside my window at the Abel Hotel. Quiet. A good time to spend time with this log. John Welch urges me to stay with it, as it will be an important public document someday, he believes. If nothing else, I can present it to him at some later date as a token of our time spent together over many breakfasts. Welch takes an extreme interest in the details of the bridge's construction. I think he would have made a fine engineer, and I've told him as much.

Excavation for the east main pier foundation was made in the same manner as outlined above, except it was not necessary to use a diver, as there was no shale to be removed in this foundation. Instead, 49-foot steel H-beam piles were driven to firm shale under this footing. The bearing capacity of the sandy material on which this footing rests is sufficient to carry the load safely, but H-beam piles were added to carry the entire load, should the foundation be fully undermined.

Before work on the east abutment foundation could progress, excavation of an approximately 20-foot section of the levee was necessary. As an advanced contingency plan, should it become necessary to protect the break in the levee—always a distinct possibility this time of year—I suggested that complete backfilling inside and outside the cofferdam would be the safest way to protect the property behind the levee and because the cofferdam is constructed of light material and is not designed for heavy duty. This method will not be costly because the amount of material involved will be small, and it will be very easy to remove the material from inside the cofferdam after the water recedes. Hopefully, this plan will not be needed.

The first steel H-beam piles were driven in the abutment foundation with a number 9-B-2 McKiernan & Terry steam hammer developing 7,000 foot-pounds of energy per blow. The 50-foot piles, as called for on the revised plans, were driven, but only 18 tons per pile bearing capacity was developed. The intent of the design was to develop approximately 50 tons per pile, so it was necessary to splice an additional 24-foot length onto the piles and drive them to hard shale.

It was now evident that the viaduct bent piles would not develop sufficient bearing capacity unless they also were driven to rock, as I had suggested when the revision of the foundation plan was made; therefore, an additional 24-foot length of pile was ordered at this time.

The contractor elected to use a bolted connection, rather than a welded connection, for splicing this additional length of pile. First, the holes in the top section of the pile were set in place and spot-welded to the section already driven; then the lower holes were drilled, the splice bolted up, and the nuts spot-welded to prevent loosening while driving.

When I inspected the first bolted splice, I found a slight opening between the two sections of the pile where the ends had not been milled square. I had this opening welded full to give perfect bearing between the ends of the piles and thus reduced the shearing stress on the bolts and prevented any eccentric loading at this point.

No difficulties were encountered in driving the piles. They were plumbed two ways with transits and driven through a timber guide at the bottom, while the top was held in position by guy ropes. In the east main pier foundation, angles were welded to the web of the pile near the top to aid in transferring the load from the foundation to the pile. All foundation piles will extend from 3 to 7 feet into the footings, fixing the top in the manner of a fixed column.

In the meantime, Stephen Shyrock—Buck, as he's so aptly called by the locals—stays on, passing to and fro over the river like a metronome set to slow; always, the knob-headed dog at his side, like it's melded to the side of his knee. The determination and resilience of the old man is staggering.

Finished for now. Welch, I hope the time and effort I'm spending on this record is worth it in the end.

CHAPTER 23

THE WARNING

Buck Shyrock hated a meddler in the worst way. John Welch knew this, and so their friendship was based upon the usual ways of men: talk about work, talk about crops, talk about the weather, talk about fishing, talk (as little as possible) about one's health. They had once discussed family and all the joys, disappointments, and misfortunes that went along with that many-layered topic (never getting into what should be left at home). But Welch had no children or grandchildren, so ever since Edna died, Shyrock never spoke of his own. Occasionally, the two of them gossiped about the town folk, even though they believed themselves above that sort of nonsense and always tried dispensing with it as quickly as possible. Beyond that, it was the usual haranguing and harassment, one suggesting to the other that he thought him to be the biggest fool the good Lord ever saw fit to make.

What Welch needed to say to Shyrock now didn't fit into any of these categories.

"Word around town is that Turner boy means you harm. And the dog." Welch put the lilt of a question on the second part, like it made no sense. As if to suggest, "Men always are wanting to cause each other harm but a *dog*?"

"That Turner boy is a pissant. A drunk and a pissant," Buck said, explaining away Welch's concern.

"A drunken pissant. The worst kind," John Welch said, lighting a cigar and looking over at the construction site from the deck of the ferry. Floyd Bailey said that once the groundwork was done, the rest would go more quickly. "Turner and them like him know they're pissants," he went on, "and they get drunk so they don't feel it quite so much. Problem is, then they get angry because they're still a pissant. The alcohol doesn't get rid of the knowing. It just turns it to poison. Makes 'em dangerous."

"I'll heed the warning," Buck said, putting it to rest.

"Please do," Welch said, plunking the cigar back in his mouth.

Welch still hadn't told his friend about his breakfast chats with the bridge engineer, and it lay heavy on his mind. He had told himself he would tell Buck, but every time he started to, it seemed ridiculous—the notion of telling a man he was having breakfast with another man. Welch could already hear Buck: "Man can have breakfast with who he pleases." So he hadn't told him. Still, it ate at Welch, like he was intentionally hiding something.

Buck looked him straight in the eye, for the first time in a long time. When *was* the last time—at Edna's funeral, when Buck had offered his sympathies? Now Welch wondered if he'd read his thoughts about the secret he was keeping, but then Shyrock said, "I seen a seagull a while back. You ever seen a seagull flyin' down the Wabash, John?"

Shyrock never called him John. It always had been "Welch" since he could remember. First grade, day one—Welch. Buck had walked up to him at school, even then using his clipped language, an economy of words, like talking was an onerous task that had to be tolerated. "Name's Stephen.

'Preciate if ya call me Buck, though. Yours?" He'd said, "Johnny Welch," suddenly ashamed of the childish sound of his own name after hearing the mature ring of *Buck*. Shyrock caught his embarrassment. "Welch. Glad ta meet ya," he said, putting out his hand like he was already a man and expected to be treated so. "Welch" it had been, ever since— through school, through fishing and netting and raking mussels when they were young; and later, through work, family, and illnesses . . . and deaths. "Welch."

"No, never have. A seagull, huh?"

"Wingin' it straight down the channel like it had a purpose." Buck still looked straight at Welch. Locked in.

Welch could see Buck had already attached a meaning to the event. "Strange," he said. "What are ya thinkin'?"

Buck looked away, down to where the seagull had disappeared from his sight, around the long, gradual bend in the river. "Yeah. Strange." Absently, he reached down and felt the dog's ear.

After that, his eyes fixed back on the river just ahead of the ferry, focused on the next thing and no further. Whatever the bird's appearance represented to him, this much was clear: it brought him no peace, no consolation, no message of hope.

At that very moment, Welch had the strangest thought. He wished the ferry would sink straightaway, to the bottom, right then and there, taking them both down with it—a blessing, saving them both a lot of trouble. Maybe they'd lived long enough.

LOG ENTRY: 4 April, 1939. All pier footings were poured before unwatering the cofferdams. A 10-inch, watertight tremie pipe, topped with a funnel-

shaped hopper holding a cubic yard of concrete, was used in the pouring. A derrick handled the tremie pipe as well as the bottom dump concrete bucket. Dowel bars extending into the footings were spot-welded into a rigid frame and lowered between guides to the correct elevation in the fresh concrete as soon as the last concrete was poured. Although these water-seal footings were designed to provide sufficient weight to prevent flotation from 100 percent hydrostatic pressure with the water level 5 feet above mean water level, the cofferdams were not unwatered until the concrete had set for 72 hours. After unwatering the cofferdams, picks and jackhammers were used to remove the laitance and level the concrete.

CHAPTER 24

THE GARDEN

After supper, Belle sent the girls outside to play and came to sit with August on the summer porch overlooking their big garden. From one end of summer to the other, she pampered and nursed the plants. On her knees, she'd pluck out the tiniest of weeds before they could get a foothold. She'd carry buckets of water, two at a time, from the house to the garden and would hoe and stake and coo to the plants like they were her children.

She handed August a bowl of strawberry-rhubarb cobbler topped with dollops of vanilla ice cream. "Fresh out of the oven," she said.

"Mmm, thanks." He held the bowl up to his nose, breathing in its tartly sweet aroma, the crust baked to a crisp golden perfection. Noticing her sitting empty-handed, August said, "Aren't you havin' any?"

"I'll have mine with the girls."

He speared his fork into the bowl, coming up with a gouge of ice cream melded to cobbler. "Belle, I don't remember the garden ever looking so fine."

"You say that every year." She raised her hands and showed him the dirt under her fingernails. "Takes work is all."

They sat quietly, both thinking of the windfall of produce that would continue coming their way throughout the summer and into the fall. Lettuce, zucchini, carrots, broccoli, cauliflower, moist cucumbers, enough tomatoes to feed an army, rows of onions rising up out of the powdery soil to sit flat on the surface, as if calling, "Here I am—what are you waiting for?" Corn, watermelon and muskmelon. Red raspberries, growing wild and unruly in their own corner patch of the garden. The autumn squash—butternut, buttercup, acorn, even hubbard and turban—too much really, much more than they could eat, but so pretty to the eye Belle couldn't resist planting them, if only for decoration. And finally, at the end of the season, August thrusting the garden fork into the chill ground, Belle at his side, having insisted once again upon harvesting the potatoes in the pale light of dusk so as to not "awaken them" too suddenly.

On the screened porch, breaking the spell, Belle said, "I saw Dad again today. Took him his dinner. Auggie, he's looking worse all the time."

"Yeah, I've noticed."

"What do we do? He's slowly wasting away, it seems like."

"Short of boxin' his ears and sayin', 'Wake up!' I don't know what to do." August sighed and shook his head. "I told you way back I had a bad feelin' about it."

Belle wanted to scream at him. *You had a bad feeling—so what!* But like the last time she had confronted him about his slackness with his father, it could only end badly. Between all she had to do to keep a household going and worrying about August's father, she didn't have the energy for it. On top of that, Holly had been acting strangely since that day she returned home from the grocery story.

Men were a helpless lot when you came right down to it. Feelings were such a mystery to them. They didn't have the faintest idea what to do with anything related to their emotions, unless it was anger. Oh yes, they could wave that around like it was a shield, deflecting anything that came close to piercing their leathery hides. And yet Belle had heard about men—boys, really—who on the battlefield cried for their mamas.

She swept a loose strand of hair into place behind her ear and stood up. "I won't let it happen," she said.

"Won't let what happen?"

Leaving the porch, Belle rolled her eyes, shook her head. So this was her helpmate. Some help!

From inside the house, August heard Belle call the girls in from the front yard for dessert and listened to the commotion that followed. Once they sat down to their bedtime treat, it grew quiet. Dusk settled softly over the expanse of garden like a blanket on a baby. As the evening dew moistened the ground, August imagined the furry roots stretching themselves awake under the soil. The plants would keep on growing and producing. Nothing except utter calamity would stop them now. They all would be fed: Holly, Vivian, Belle, and him . . . and the old man—yes, the old man. Belle would see to it.

LOG ENTRY: 7 July, 1939. Each main pier consists of two round, reinforced concrete columns connected at the top by a reinforced concrete strut. These columns are 8 feet in diameter at the footing and 7 feet in diameter at the top. The lower section of these pier columns was given two coats of Inertol, a waterproofing preparation.

The anchor pier is similar to the main pier except the columns are square and smaller. These columns are 5½ feet square at the footing and 4 feet square at the top. The main function of this pier is to resist the uplift caused by the vertical component of the cable pull.

All forms for concrete were built up in sections at the site and set in place either by hand or by the derricks. The forms were made of ¾-inch siding on 2x6-inch studding and were secured in place by 3/8-inch tie rods. Above the ground line, the forms were lined with ¼-inch plywood over ¾-inch siding to give a smoother finish to the concrete. Exposed concrete surfaces were rubbed with a carborundum stone as soon as the forms were removed and will be given a final rubbing just before the contract is completed.

The concrete mix was designed by a testing laboratory. Grade B concrete was a nominal 1:6 mix containing a minimum of 5.64 bags of cement per cubic yard and having a minimum compressive strength of 2,600 pounds at 28 days. Grade A concrete will be used in thin walls and the floor, with a nominal 1:3 mix containing a minimum of 6.16 bags of cement per cubic yard and having a compressive strength of 3,200 pounds at 28 days. Sample cylinders, made for each 250 cubic yards of concrete as a check on the quality of the concrete, broke as high as 4,600 pounds, and all broke well above the required strength. Careful control of the concrete was maintained by weighing all aggregate. The concrete above the water seal was placed through metal tremies and puddled in the forms by mechanical vibrators.

The viaduct bents consist of two 94-foot, 12-inch, 49-pound steel H-beam piles driven about 75 feet to practical refusal into shale and framed together above the ground by steel struts and braces. The piles were cut off at the correct elevation and a polished bronze bearing plate for supporting the girder was welded on the top of each pile. A vertical pin in this bearing plate will fit into a slotted hole in a similar bearing plate on the bottom of the girder. The hole will be slotted so the girder can move longitudinally but not transversely. Any movement of the span due to temperature changes will cause the girder to slide on these bronze bearing plates and thus not transfer undue bending to the pile bent.

CHAPTER 25

SAFE PASSAGE

Buck Shyrock had an unblemished safety record. Once, a truck loaded with poultry had driven off the front river-end of the ferry, snapping the barrier chain and drowning every single chicken, but no one blamed Buck for that. The truck's brakes had failed.

Crossing the river, the ferry always had the right-of-way. Cumbersome, tethered to the cable, and carrying a load to boot, it wasn't possible for it turn or to stop suddenly to avoid a collision. Other watercraft, mostly fishermen in johnboats on this stretch of the river, were to give the ferry wide berth.

An uprooted oak tree, its wilting leaves still clinging to the thick branches, was another matter entirely.

The nearly submerged tree moved steadily with the current. Only the upper limbs were visible, but their reach hinted at the massive girth of the trunk below. A long, suctioning trough of water at the back, trailing the tree's sunken root mass, made sucking and smacking noises like a great toothless maw, pulling in all that was around it: leaves and sticks; brown, frothy bubbles floating in a milky scum; a sheet of paper, still intact; a gray, filthy sock hung up on a rotting piece of driftwood; a clear, floating bottle, empty but with its cork intact.

The men on the bridge crew saw it first. The river's tree-lined bank and sudden twist to the south kept it hidden from view until, suddenly, it was *"There!"* in the relatively straight section of river where they were working. A single falsework timber pile, fifty feet or so out from the Illinois riverbank, held the end weight of the first two steel girders erected. Fortunately, the advancing colossus was well out into the center of the current, so their timber pile appeared to be safe from harm. They whistled and shouted to one another, pointing and calling, "Look there! Hey! Hey! Can you believe that!"

The retirees took up the call. Chester Howe yipped and ballyhooed, waving his hat above his head as if at a rodeo. They all watched in awe as the giant tree headed dead-center down the middle of the river, past where they stood. One by one, in rapid succession, they thought of the ferry and looked down toward the ferry crossing.

There was the old man, stoic as always, standing firmly in the steer boat as if part tree himself, just setting off toward the Indiana bank. Two cars were on board. Quick mental reckoning showed a collision at mid-river to be a near certainty. They quickly shut down the diesel engine that powered the derrick. Workers and retirees alike began hollering and waving their arms. A couple of them whistled shrilly through their fingers to try to get Shyrock's attention. The old men, those who were able, began tripping and staggering along the high riverbank, hoping Buck would turn his head and see them. But he kept looking straight ahead, oblivious.

How best to explain a seasoned river man, intimately familiar with the river's penchant for surprises and sudden hazards, failing to spot the giant oak? Simply stated, because of the constant brouhaha of the unwelcome bridge construction, the edge had worn off Buck's peripheral world. He remained unaware until his passengers, out of their cars and gazing up at the bridge site, started dancing and scurrying around on the deck, making frightened bird noises. Buck finally saw it—massive in its reach and bobbing up and down in the current in a slow, lazy motion. Its forward velocity, however, was anything but slow and lazy. The tree was no more than a hundred fifty to two hundred feet away.

Buck knew he couldn't beat it, so he cut the throttle, jammed the boat into neutral and, after waiting just a few seconds for it to lose rpms, forced it into reverse with a sickening grinding of gears. Hailing back to the pre-motor days, he resorted to a tried-and-true method used by the old cable ferrymen and taught to him by his father—back then, it was their only means of propulsion. Gunning the engine, he quickly forced the stern backward into the current so the ferry hovered at an angle, the bow a bit downriver. In this way, Shyrock intended to use the current's considerable force to help propel the ferryboat backward out of the tree's path, more quickly than the motor alone could have done. It immediately began scuttling backward as Buck wanted, but the tree was moving faster.

A passenger traveling alone jumped into his car at the front of the ferry. Stumbling from the sudden shift in direction, the parents from the other vehicle grabbed up their children and glanced frantically around before darting toward Buck at the far corner of the ferry farthest away from the limbs. Children in hand, they dropped to the deck and grasped the railing next to Shyrock.

Miraculously, no one was injured. Limbs raked across the bow, snapping off both rails, and with a loud, sickening screech left a ragged, open gash across the hood of the gentleman's car. Buck saw the man cover his face and duck into his seat just as the end of a limb slammed against his driver's side window, shattering it to pieces. The children screamed and cried, and their mother and father stared at Shyrock in disbelief, as though he'd gone mad. Rebel made such a terrible racket that Buck had to put his hand around her snout to get her to stop. As the tree traveled on down the river, Buck stared at it with a mixture of awe and total befuddlement. He had seen all manner of strange and unbelievable sights during his years on the river. Not having seen this one is what confounded him.

As expected, the news quickly made its circuit around Millerville. People came to see for themselves the splintered rails and the long, crooked scrapes across the bow. "Close one there, Buck," one gawker said, elbowing his neighbor, barely able to conceal his glee at facing the man who was, once again, the source of much excitement for the town— first the drowned man, now this.

Dorothy Smith wrote about it in Millerville's weekly, of course—"Tragedy Barely Averted" was the headline on the front page, with a close-up of the crushed railings underneath. It even got coverage in the *Robinson Daily*, not to mention the Sullivan papers. There were plenty of eyewitnesses to retell the story, though Buck flatly refused interviews and told the camera-toting Dorothy he didn't trust her to tell any part of the truth. Speaking that word, *truth*, it occurred to him that even he wasn't sure exactly what had happened. When she aimed the camera his way, Buck told her in no uncertain terms that if she ever took another picture of him while the breath of life was still in him, he'd chuck her camera in the river.

The sensation even drew a visit from Faber McNutt, who made it a rule to leave the ferrying end of things to Shyrock. He despised the sodden, fishy smell of the river and its banks, and besides, he was deathly afraid of water.

Without so much as a greeting, he appeared at the bottom end of the ferry landing, out of breath and perspiring heavily from his walk. He moved just close enough to the river's edge to get a look at the damage done to his property, no doubt with an eye to replacement costs. Buck stood beside him, his head tucked into his shoulders, not defeated exactly, but battered and humiliated nonetheless. An old, resident look of stubbornness remained.

McNutt removed his hat and swiped the top of his bald head and face with a handkerchief. "What the blazes, Shyrock? What were you thinking, man?" he panted.

Buck grappled with the question. It was a fair one, and McNutt deserved an answer, but what do you say when there just isn't one? Besides, Buck wasn't accustomed to answering to anyone in relation to his work. His last experience of that was with his father, who had been gone too long now for Buck to recall what it meant to be accountable to someone. In respect to his vocation, his answers always came in the form of actions. When someone showed up needing transport across the river, regardless of the time of day or the weather, his response was to provide it. On Saturdays, he carried the receipts bag to McNutt and returned to the ferry with it empty. Except as it related to his interaction with the river, he did what he did without much thought, and there was never a need for answers. He crossed from one side of the river to the other, the way water fowl cross the miles when migrating with the seasons—instinctively. And now his instincts seemed to have failed him.

Since his answers always equated to action, he said, "I can fix it back up. Be done before ya know it." It was all he knew to say.

McNutt waved him off impatiently. Didn't the ferryman understand the magnitude of the problem? "There'll be a letter from the *state*," he huffed, watching the water out of the corner of his eye as it lapped at the landing. His indoor complexion was even paler than usual, as if he feared the river might suddenly grab him by the ankle and pull him in. "Safe passage, Shyrock, safe passage! You know what this means!"

Shyrock knew. The state issued the license to operate the ferry, and the state could take it away. No doubt about it; someone would be sent to investigate.

"If you can't give *me* an answer, Shyrock, you damn well better think of an answer for *them*."

In a hurry to get away from the river, McNutt looked briefly at the progress being made on the bridge. "Hmm, interesting," he mumbled. He turned on his heel and struggled slowly up the incline the landing. Leaning forward, stiff-legged, he held a hand to his hip like a man not used to physical exertion.

Shyrock watched him go. Oddly, he felt sorry for the man and his physical weakness and that he had caused him worry. He did feel bad that he couldn't answer McNutt's query. Yes, he deserved an answer. Worse yet, Shyrock had to answer to himself.

More than anything, Buck felt bad about scaring the children.

In the end, the state did send a man to investigate. Buck couldn't provide an answer to him any more than he could to McNutt. While Buck stood looking at his feet, waiting for some kind of words, any words, to dislodge themselves from his brain, McNutt came up with a barely plausible excuse himself. It involved the rapidness of the current, the way the "suddenly visible" tree appeared out of nowhere. He described it in such a way, counter to all other reports, that it was as though the tree had remained submerged and only surfaced when almost upon the ferry. He ended by expounding, at some length, on the ferry's perfect safety record. He promised to take a more involved role in the ferry's daily operation.

Just then, a sudden breeze started from up the river and as it traveled southward, it stirred the leaves of the trees all up and down both banks. Their rustling sounded like applause—pretty near a standing ovation. Buck turned an ear to the river to see if it, too, would respond and maybe speak in his defense in some way. Nothing came. The sun reflected off its silent, dappled surface and shone like a spotlight on the dancing leaves across the way.

The decision that came down from Springfield was to issue a warning. Everyone knew it was the only course that made sense, considering the bridge would be completed within the year. The license became a provisional one.

Dorothy Smith wouldn't let it rest. In the *Gazette*, she demanded a "word of apology and of reassurance."

"It is the least Mr. McNutt and his agent, Mr. Shyrock, can do," she wrote, "considering the untold trauma inflicted upon the passengers, including innocent children, and to the community at large in the form of lost confidence in the ferry as a mode of safe travel."

Word of her rant got back to Buck. If it had been anyone else asking—one of the passengers, say—Buck would have apologized in a minute. Lying on his bed, rolling the whole grisly, near-catastrophe over in his mind, he yawned and then released a long, hoarse sigh. "I wouldn't apologize now if it was my death bed I's lyin' on," he said aloud. Did the river offer apologies? Had it ever?

His big hand reached over the side of the bed and touched the dog's ribs. They rose and then lowered again, slowly, steadily. She sneezed and then licked the end of her nose.

"Wanna trade places? I'll be the dog for a while." He waited as if he truly expected an answer and then chuckled joylessly. "'Course not. You're way too smart for that."

He thought of Ida. "I'm sorry, Ida, 'specially for the little ones," he murmured, almost asleep now. And then, after a moment: "If ever I needed you, I need you now."

≈ ≈ ≈

John Welch's reaction to the news was immediate. The very next day he would call it off with Floyd Bailey. No more breakfasts, no more talk of the bridge. Why make a new friend if you can't stick by your old one?

Progress or no progress.

CHAPTER 26

SOME SMALL DIFFERENCE

Five-thirty in the morning and already it was hot—steamy and close, air so thick you would rather not have to drag it into your lungs. The early heat portended a day in which relief would not easily be found.

John Welch would rather have planted himself under the giant old maples festooning his side yard. With their deep shade, they were a weather system unto themselves. He had escaped the stifling confines of the house before sunrise and, except for throwing corn to the cows, would have been perfectly content to stay put under that canopy of cool air and muted light the entire day. But he had told himself today was the day to make his announcement to Floyd.

Floyd was a decent fellow. If anyone would get it, he would. Floyd, Welch was sure, knew the meaning and value of friendship. He didn't dread talking to him as much as he simply hated to do it. A project the size and complexity of the Millerville bridge excited Welch, no two ways around it. It was a once-in-a-lifetime event, and he, "Farmer John" from Millerville, Illinois, had a private audience with a man in the very thick of it. It was gratifying to talk with someone who loved his work as much as Floyd did. Watching Floyd get excited about the upcoming day's tasks was an experience itself and started Welch's day with a welcome spark.

Welch traipsed slowly to the house for his hat, trying to avoid working up a sweat once he was out of the shade. Within moments, he was glowing like a firefly. By the time he'd hauled himself into the truck, his shirt was wet under the arms, the rest of him dampening quickly. Driving from his place, John looked back at the shade longingly. "I'll be back in a jiffy," he said to the old trees.

Once out on the gravel, Welch jammed the wing vent on the driver's side open all the way and flapped the sides of his yet-unbuttoned bib overalls. The corn, at least, loved this weather. It grew noticeably by the day. Watching the fields glide by outside his window, stretched out in gently rolling mounds that his father had called hillocks, Welch reminded himself he was a farmer first and foremost, and that he was doing the right thing in backing away from Floyd Bailey. He had no business fancying himself as knowing the first thing about bridge building anyway. Yes, a farmer—same as Shyrock was a ferry operator—and nothing more. *We are born to what the good Lord intended for us.* Floyd Bailey, the engineer, was born to that.

Floyd sat at his usual station, the counter stool closest to the door. It was like he knew his place in the stew mix that was Millerville. He could step inside the door, have a seat, and greet folks, but he could never truly blend in with the locals, certainly not in a matter of a few hundred days. After several months of coming to the same place for breakfast every day, he still felt the intruder. Welch had tried to entice him to a booth near the back once, but he'd responded with, "This is fine. I like the light from the window." As a result, Welch's assigned seat had become the second from the door. No one sat on John Welch's bar stool when Floyd Bailey occupied the first.

Floyd had coffee in front of him but had waited for Welch to arrive before ordering his breakfast. Before Welch could greet him, Sal was standing in front of them. "Okay, Captain, you first," she said, smiling at Floyd, her pencil stub and order pad at the ready. No matter how many times a customer ordered the exact same meal, Sal considered it a breach of professional standards to deny anyone the privilege of placing an order and having it recorded.

After Floyd ordered, she looked at Welch. "And you, Lieutenant?" Over time, Sal had come up with her own terms for them, the teacher and the understudy—Captain and Lieutenant.

"I'll have pickled octopus on a bed of wild rice, graced by a smattering of fresh chives," Welch said, trying to lighten his mood.

"Been reading the society pages in the Terre Haute paper again, I see," Sal said. "How 'bout fried channel cat dropped onto a mess of grill-fried onions and scrambled eggs, ketchup on the side?"

"Perfect. Isn't that what I said?"

She slid the pencil stub behind her ear and turned on her heel to leave them. "Carry on with your battle plans, gentlemen," she said over her shoulder.

"Blessed hot," Welch said to Floyd.

"Only the beginning. The bridge iron will be scalding before we get halfway to noon. Can't sit on it, can't hardly touch it, even with gloves."

"Ouch," Welch said sympathetically.

Although all the timber pile clusters and steel girders had yet to be put into place, Floyd was anxious to jump ahead and talk about cabling. "This is a very critical and exciting part of the bridge assembly," he said, not wasting any time, as if Welch was a member of the crew, and he was eager for him to get started. "When finished, each of the two main cables will be made up of nine strands of one-and-half-inch-diameter wire rope." Floyd used his finger and thumb to show about how thick the strands would be. "Each strand will consist of fifty-one wires varying from point-one-zero inch to point one-nine-six inches in diameter. The ultimate strength per strand will be two hundred seventy thousand pounds."

"Hmm. Sounds strong enough," John said, raising his eyebrows but with halfhearted interest.

Floyd stated the numbers and dimensions of the suspender cables and then launched into explaining how the erection of the cabling would be "relatively simple, but a lot could go wrong."

"Simple for you," Welch said, his voice showing a faint hint of irritation at how Floyd rattled on. He wondered about main cables versus suspender cables but didn't interrupt Floyd to ask. At this point, did it matter that he know this minor detail?

Floyd hesitated, glanced at him, and then continued.

He went on to explain how, as a first step, a reel would be set up on each of the towers, now under construction, and at the center of the main span; and then how, strand by strand, the wire rope would be pulled across the bridge structure by a small cable attached to a reel on a gasoline hoisting engine. He was explaining how a tag line attached to a lever on the reel would keep the cable from twisting during erection, when he suddenly stopped in midsentence and looked inquisitively at Welch. "John, you're not with me."

"Floyd, I'm sorry. I haven't been with you for some time."

"You look troubled."

"I am. I am troubled," he said, nodding. "Floyd, I am very troubled."

Floyd sat quietly, waiting for him to offer an explanation.

"My friend, you have been very kind to me. And very patient," Welch began. "I'm afraid I'm a bit of a dullard when it comes to all this." He waved his arm tiredly in the air.

"Not at all, John. Like I told you before, you would make a fine structural engineer."

"But I'm not a structural engineer, Floyd. This whole time, since we met, I've probably understood a fifth of what you've said. If that." He looked at Floyd apologetically, embarrassed by himself. "Mostly, I've nodded my head to keep you talking. The parts I've understood have been fascinating. The majority has been listening to a man who loves his work. There's worse ways to pass my time, you know."

Floyd's face softened. "You are very kind yourself, John. But I'm afraid you flatter me."

"I'm beyond flattering anyone. Flattery is the guise of those who think they have something to gain. At this point in my life, I have nothing to gain. Only things to lose."

"John, you don't have to explain any more. I understand completely." He held up his coffee cup between them as if offering a toast. "You are needed elsewhere."

At a loss, Welch clinked his cup against Floyd's. "You . . . understand. What do you understand? I haven't said anything yet."

"You don't have to. You're his friend. It's only natural. In your position, I would do the same thing." He nodded. "Yes, hopefully, I would do the same thing."

Welch still found it hard to believe—Floyd reading his mind? "*What* would you do?"

Sal slid their plates in front of them in unison but didn't interrupt. Politely, she looked away, sensing the intensity of their conversation. Floyd gazed at his plate of food a long while and then gave his eggs a good peppering. Finally, he shrugged his shoulders. "Look," he said. "I saw the whole thing."

"The tree mishap, you mean."

"Yep. If I were you, I'd give me the toss and devote my attention to my friend."

Welch winced at Floyd's choice of phrase, about giving him *the toss*. "It won't change nothin'," Welch said. "Not a thing."

"It'll make a difference to Stephen Shyrock."

His elbows on the counter, his head tucked into his shoulders, Welch sat and stared at his breakfast. "That's what I'm hopin', I reckon," he said, fully resigned now to giving Floyd "the toss," knowing what he said was true. "Some small difference, maybe."

The two men poked at their breakfasts in silence. There was no more talk of the bridge. Outside the window, the day heated up. Main Street sent up little wavy flags of simmering moisture from the bitumen; the flat roofs across the way steamed as if ready to combust into flames. Through the screen door, heat soughed in and lay on the men's backs, slouching them at the shoulders. Two soggy-looking people, an old man and a woman who looked to be his daughter, yanked open the door and walked halfway down the counter into the otherwise empty café before she emitted a single "ugh" and shook her head. They left, the old fella trailing her, with his small, wrinkled head tipped forward on his neck, not looking to either side. Sal, leaning against the glass-topped box cooler where she kept the soda pop in ice-cold water at the far end of the counter, shrugged her shoulders and went back to filing her nails.

Finally, his breakfast little more than mussed piles, John Welch straightened his back. "Never thought I'd hear myself say it's too hot to eat," he said.

"See you at the bridge dedication then?" Floyd wanted to make it easy for him.

"Yep, reckon I'll be there somewhere. Already predictin' a crowd, I hear. Not sure you'll find me."

"I'll find you, John," the bridge engineer said kindly.

Before sliding off his stool, Welch jammed his hand into Floyd's, not quite looking him in the eye. He mumbled something that Floyd didn't quite catch before he lumbered out the door, as if it was yet another day coming his way to be met like every other day—staying open to the minor possibilities and ready to face up to its major pitfalls.

By a slowly rising flush at the back of his neck, Floyd Bailey felt the beginnings of joy going out of his day. And they hadn't even gotten around to telling war stories.

CHAPTER 27

A NAUGHTY GIRL

Holly needed to convince her mother that she was ready to go back to town on her own. She still hadn't been able to explain what had happened that last time when she was sent for bread and came home empty-handed. Although clearly worried, her mother hadn't pursued it.

Recently, while Vivian was distracted by a neighbor girl, Holly had tiptoed around the house to stand next to the summer porch wall. She had overheard her mother telling her father that she was worried about Gramps, that he didn't look well. "Wasting away," she'd called it. Her father had said he had a "bad feeling."

Holly had returned to the front yard with a sense of doom weighing on her chest. She'd hardly slept at all that night, the memory of her terrifying vision replaying in her head over and over.

She had to see for herself, without her Gramps knowing she was watching, so he wouldn't be putting on a happy face for her benefit. If he looked okay to her, then what she'd seen at the grocery store was just a "brain spell," as she'd sometimes come to think of it when trying to put it out of her mind. Her mother worried too much. Her father even said so.

"All right, sweetie. If you're sure you're ready," her mother said, fishing through her coin purse. She held the quarter, suspended above Holly's open hand. "You sure?"

"Yes, Mother, I'm sure." Up until now, Holly had always called her "Mommy," but she wanted to impress upon her how grown-up she was getting.

Noticing, Belle raised an eyebrow but didn't comment. She laid the coin in Holly's open palm. "Okay, a loaf of bread and a dozen eggs. Come straight home."

Holly nodded her head confidently, a firm single nod, and started out.

She hadn't yet worked out how she would remain unseen while trying to get a good look at her Gramps. Her only plan was to go somewhere near the ferry landing first, before she went to the grocery store. She was afraid that the longer she waited, the more chance there was she would lose her nerve. Disobeying her mother was not something she wanted to do. And under the watchful eye of Mr. Abel, who had a way of looking at her like he was trying to read her thoughts, she might change her mind.

The grocery store, she thought with a shiver. She hadn't been back, even with her mom, since the "brain spell" had happened.

Holly had no trouble finding a place to hide. A strip of leafy brush claimed the space between the south edge of the ferry landing and the nearest house. The strip was wide enough for Holly to pass through it unseen from either direction. By bending down at the waist, she made it through the undergrowth with little impediment, except for the mosquitoes. They attacked her, ravenously, almost covering her in a matter of seconds. She tried brushing them aside with her arm, but they buzzed her face, bumping against her eyelids, flailing around inside her ears, biting, biting, biting her. There seemed to be thousands of them. For every one she flattened against her skin, three or four more seemed to take its place. Persisting, she made her way to a gigantic tree, from which she had a clear view of the ferry landing and the wide river itself. The tree's trunk was so big around that she could hide behind it and be invisible.

Between swatting and slapping at her own skin, mindful not to make too much noise, Holly listened for her grandfather, who as yet was nowhere to be seen. Then, across the river, over by where the sandbank had been packed down into a car path sloping to the water's edge, a long, shiny black car crested the levee, and already was laying on its horn. A few moments later, Holly heard her grandpa's screen door creak open and then snap back on its spring. She crept out just far enough to peek around the tree. There he was—Rebel, too—opposite the gullied-out landing approach, almost at eye level. As he stepped down off the porch, he glanced her way, a curious look passing over his face. She ducked her head back behind the tree. He made his way around to the top end of the landing and then down its slope without looking her way again. Good; he hadn't seen her.

Her grandfather untied the ferry and lowered himself into the steer boat behind Rebel. She was close enough to hear him grunt with the effort. With a single pull at the rope, the motor shivered, and a white exhaust cloud floated away from the boat and over the water. Her grandfather fiddled with the motor until it finally juddered to life.

Thirty feet or so from shore, he turned and looked her way again. She hadn't expected it and had her head out from behind the tree. He had seen her for sure. Now she was in big trouble.

She turned and stumbled out of the undergrowth, back the way she'd come. The air felt cool on her face when she burst into the open, still flailing at the mosquitoes that had pursued her out of the brushy enclosure. She hadn't gotten a good look at her Gramps, so busy was she trying to stay hidden while not getting eaten alive. Whether he was "wasting away," she still wasn't sure. What did someone who was wasting away look like, anyway? Holly was more concerned now with the trouble she was going to be in for getting too close to the river and for not going straight to the store, like she was told.

At the store, Mr. Abel was busy behind the meat counter and didn't seem to notice her. Avoiding the cereal aisle, she snatched the bread off the shelf and yanked a carton of eggs off a table without stopping. If she ran home, making it look like she had done exactly as she'd been told, she could deny it was her at the river. It must have been some other girl lurking about there—*a naughty girl*.

CHAPTER 28

MONKEY CAKE

For her fourth birthday party, Vivian was locked in high gear. She ran from room to room, singing "Happy buhthday to me!" over and over. Belle tried to corral her, telling her, "No running in Gramps's house," but Vivian couldn't contain herself more than a few seconds before she was at it again. From his chair in the kitchen, Buck tried to grab her each time she shot past close enough for him to touch her dress, but she ducked and dodged, giggling and slipping through his arms like a wisp of smoke.

When August sternly told her to stop, to listen to her mother, Buck intervened. "Oh, let her run. This house needs the dust shaken loose." He could tell August didn't like him saying it—he'd see it as questioning his and Belle's authority—so he didn't say any more. But he caught the quick look—*Let it go*—that passed from Belle to August.

Making another run through the kitchen, Vivian called out to Rebel to follow. The hound lay next to Buck, watching from under the table, her ears springing up with puzzlement and minor alarm each time the child passed.

When the dog refused to move, Vivian called to her sister, looking back over her shoulder as she charged into the parlor, "C'mon, Hawwy, do it wif me!"

Holly ignored her. She was focused on trying to act natural around her granddad. She had been back to the ferry landing twice more, hiding in the mosquito-filled brush like a bandit. She thought for sure her Gramps had seen her all three times, but if he had, wouldn't he have said something to her mom and dad that she was going to a place they had forbidden? *Stay away from the river*, they had always told her, making it clear the danger that was involved. She felt a little more emboldened each time she got away with it. It was an unexpected feeling, one she'd never had before. Being *the naughty girl.* It made her skin tingle and her breath come a little quicker. But still, she hadn't stopped worrying about him—*really* worrying. That was the biggest—in fact, the only—reason for her stopovers at the river.

Her Gramps acted the same as always, pulling her to his side just now when she walked shyly up to him and receiving her kiss on his cheek.

"How's my Lollipop?" he asked. Buck noticed the mosquito bites speckling her neck and arms, running all up and down her legs, but he didn't say anything for fear of bringing attention to it and somehow giving away her secret—*their secret.* Belle and August would have had to notice. He wondered how she had explained the bites to them.

"Good," she said. She glanced furtively at his eyes, and he winked at her. *What did it mean? Was he telling her that he knew about her visits to the landing? Or was he just being Gramps?* Rattled, she made a show of petting the dog and then moved to her mother's side at the counter.

"Mother, can I help you?

"Yes, sweetheart. Put the candles on Viv's cake, please." Belle handed her an unopened box of pink candles.

Watching from his chair, Buck said teasingly, "Belle, you sure she can count that far? I couldn't count to four until I was almost grown."

Holly looked up at her mother, smiling uncertainly, but letting her know she got the joke.

"Dad, you probably knew how to count to a hundred by the time you were three," Belle said. "Mom told me your mother said you were a very smart little boy."

Sitting and taking it all in, still a little miffed at his father about Vivian's running in the house, August nodded his head. "I heard her say it," he agreed, feeling the need to say something. Belle would be after him later for not talking, for not letting it go.

"Oh, I dunno. I think the girls have me beat by a long sight." Just then, Vivian ran by him, getting close, tempting him but trying to evade his reach. Her quickness was diminished by all the dashing about, and Buck grabbed her and pulled her to him, tickling her ribs. "You're a smart one, ain't ya, birthday girl?"

"I'm smawter than evwybawdy!" she yelled, wriggling like a fish in his arms.

"Smarter than your sister?" he said. Buck winked at Holly again, seeing that she was watching them.

"I *said*, I'm smawter than evwybawdy!" Vivian insisted.

"Okay, Little Miss Too Loud," Belle said, giving her the shush sign. Belle had a hard time being strict with Vivian on her birthday. Plus, Dad was obviously pleased, noise or not, that they'd moved Vivian's party to his house. Belle hadn't seen him this relaxed and happy for some time.

"Cake's almost ready," Belle said. "Get me the matches from over by the stove, will you, Auggie?"

"They're on the middle shelf there, son," Buck said, pointing. "What kinda cake you havin', Viv?" Against the flat of his hand he could feel her little heart beating a fast rhythm through the back of her frilly yellow birthday dress. The tiny pulse rippling against his palm took his breath away for a moment. Everything a person needed to know and feel about what was good in this life was contained in that little *whumpa-whumpa* pressing bravely into the calluses of his hand. Things like happiness, vitality, abundance, fortitude, love, God. He thought of Ida and their lost little girl. If he could bring his wife back right now, just for this moment, he would lay her hand on little Vivian's back, so she could feel it. Without words being spoken, they would both know.

"Monkey cake!" Vivian said.

"Monkey cake! I never even heard o' monkey cake," he said, lifting her onto his lap. He looked around at everyone. "No monkeys here."

"You! Yo' a monkey, Gwamps," she said, losing herself in a fit of giggling, heaving all her weight backwards against his arm.

"If I'm a monkey, that makes *you* a monkey too, 'cause I'm your granddaddy. Gramps's little monkey, you are."

Holly carried the lighted cake to the table and set it down in front of Vivian and Buck.

"Now we get to see how windy you are," Buck said.

Vivian took a big, deep, dramatic breath, puffing up her cheeks.

"Not yet," Belle said quickly. "First we sing 'Happy Birthday.' Lolli, get us started."

Holly started singing and the grownups struggled to catch up to her, reaching for the tempo and pitch with varying degrees of success. Belle got there before the first line was finished; August eventually picked up the tempo but not the pitch, and Buck got neither. On they went, wading in fits and starts through the simple happy song. Holly and Belle glanced around, waiting for the men to fall into place, until finally the song was done, and they all looked surprised that they'd actually made it to the end.

Vivian didn't seem to notice or care that the song in honor of her big day had been butchered almost beyond recognition. Her eyes shone, reflecting the glow of the candles, and she clapped her hands with joy and excitement.

"*Now* it's time to blow out the candles," August said.

"Make a wish," Belle said, standing behind Holly, her hands on her shoulders.

"I wish that my Gwamps wasn't a monkey," Vivian said, giggling again, looking over her shoulder at Buck.

"No, a wish for yourself, silly," Buck said. "Somethin' you want to come true for yourself."

"And you can't tell anyone," Holly warned, breaking her silence, "or it won't come true."

Vivian looked at her sister, her face serious, as if she had just been assigned some grave task that she wasn't at all sure she would perform correctly. She looked at the ceiling, her brow furrowed in concentration. Suddenly, her face cleared and she leaned forward and blew air and spittle over the top of the cake, managing to blast out three of the candles. The fourth leaned a little to the side, faltering, but it didn't go completely out. Vivian sucked in a quick breath and finished what she'd started. She clapped her hands and shrieked. Everyone clapped with her except Holly, who stood up on her toes and started to protest that she hadn't blown out the candles with one breath, but Belle headed her off with a squeeze of the shoulders.

Once the candles were pulled out, Vivian chose a center piece, and Holly wanted a corner piece. They all had ice cream with their cake.

Afterward, Vivian ripped her way through the presents—a doll from August and Belle, a set of crayons from Holly. Buck had bought her a straw hat at the hardware store that had two ribbons, one pink and one yellow, dangling down the back. Faber McNutt's wife, Helen, had wrapped it for him.

"Look!" Vivian said. "The yellow one is the coluh of my dwess, and the pink one is the coluh of my buhthday candles!"

"Good job, Gramps," Belle said, clapping him on the shoulder. Buck smiled, his face all aglow, happy with his selection.

Vivian wore the hat the remainder of the summer, taking it off only to sleep and bathe—and then only because Bell convinced her it would ruin the hat's shape. "It's my buhthday pwesent fwom my Gwamps," she told everyone.

As they were leaving, Buck leaned into Holly, who lagged behind on the porch, and whispered, "You be careful, Lol. I don't want nothin' happenin' to my girl."

She didn't respond, didn't even look at him, but Buck could tell by the way she stiffened that she understood.

LOG ENTRY: 24 August, 1939. The girder spans are being erected on timber falsework bents supported on timber pile clusters set an average of 50 feet apart. Erection started at both ends of the suspended spans, and closure will be made in the main span near the Indiana tower. The girders are set one foot above dead-load position through their entire length, and their riveting—now in progress—will be completed before they are lowered into place. Their current position will also facilitate connecting the suspension cables, using timber gallows frames set on top of the towers.

Both anchor spans were erected by derricks working from the ground. A small 8-ton derrick, working on top of the steel superstructure, erected the main span. Steel was carried to the derrick on a small barge.

All steel in the bridge is structural carbon steel, except in the stiffening girders and floor beams (yet to be added), where silicon steel is required. (As mentioned earlier in this log, and it is worth repeating to understand the bridge's unique design, silicon steel is fabricated at the mill to tolerate both compressive as well as tensile force.) The stiffening girders are 36-inch beams, some of which weigh 300 pounds per foot, the heaviest rolled section made. Although the Millerville bridge is the fifth suspension bridge of the self-anchored type in the United States, it contains the longest span in which single rolled beams have been employed as stiffening girders. To an engineer, the main spans of this bridge are more interesting than the substructure or viaduct spans, which are a variation of standard type bridge construction.

I've also forgotten to mention an important detail: the tower bracing is in the form of the cross of St. George. Yet another element of grandeur in this imposing architectural piece.

I miss sharing the details of my work with John Welch. It is like I have lost a colleague who reflected back to me my own fervor for the job. As a result, some of the spark and start has gone out of my days. When I think about the arduous (impossible?) task ahead of him, helping the ferry operator transition to a new way of life . . . To have a friend like John . . . if only Stephen Shyrock could see it, his load would be lessened.

CHAPTER 29

YA AIN'T BORROWIN' MY DOG

"You been hangin' around a lot of late."

"Maybe I'm bored. You ever think o' that?"

"Next you'll be tellin' me yer lonesome."

"Well, if I *was* lonesome, I damn sure wouldn't come 'round here. I can get more conversation outta a tree."

Hanging around a lot lately meant that John Welch had shown up at Shyrock's exactly four times since his final talk with Floyd Bailey. This was a new thing. Almost all of their contact in the last several years, except the chance meeting on Main Street, had been in association with the ferry crossing.

Shyrock wasn't sure yet whether he liked it. This was the first time he'd actually let Welch in the house.

Welch looked around the kitchen and leaned forward in his chair to have a peek at the sitting room. "You're a better housekeeper than I'd a-thought."

"They's only me." Buck was hesitant to admit that his daughter-in-law cleaned his house for him, especially since he knew that Welch was a fastidious housekeeper. You'd never know it by looking at him: stained overalls, a chaw of tobacco or a cigar stuck in his yaw most of the time, more teeth missing than present. Whether he'd be clean-shaven when you next saw him seemed a matter of chance. But he had heard from a plumber who crossed on the ferry now and again and who had done work at Welch's house that you could eat off his floor.

Suddenly, Shyrock slapped his hand down on the table.

"Oh well, if you gotta know, ya nosey bastard, Belle cleans it for me every other week." In the end he had decided that Belle should get credit for her hard work, not him. Shyrock figured Welch would rib him about it, but surprisingly, he didn't.

"That's real nice of her," Welch said. "Awful nice. You're a lucky man to have her as family."

"Yeah, I am. Now mind yer own damn business."

"I'll see if I can arrange it," Welch said.

What Buck didn't tell Welch was that Belle also brought him dinner twice a week.

The two men sat quietly for a while, deep in their own thoughts. The house was brighter than it had been since Ida died—the shades open, the windows clean. Belle had worked so hard on getting the glass spotless that Shyrock kept the shades up just to show his appreciation and that he noticed what she had done, should she show up unexpectedly. Then he thought about Holly. He came close to asking Welch for advice on how to deal with his granddaughter's "secret" trips to the riverside, but including him might complicate matters. Welch would surely say he had to tell her parents because she might get hurt. Buck wasn't ready for that move, so he kept quiet about it.

Looking down at Rebel taking advantage of a strip of sunlight that stretched across the wood floor, Buck broke the silence. "You need a dog," he said.

"A dog. Why do I need a dog?"

"You said you were lonesome."

"I didn't say it. You said it. I said maybe I'm bored."

"Well, a dog'd be good for ya."

"Sayin' I do need a dog, where would I find one?"

Shyrock was stumped. He had never gone looking for one. Rebel had found him. "Ask around, I reckon. Gotta be some bitch holdin' whelps."

"I dunno."

"Do what pleases ya. But ya ain't borrowin' my dog."

"You tryin' to get rid o' me?"

"I can get used to most things."

"You mind if I borrow another cup o' that sludge you call coffee?" Welch shot back as he got up to serve himself.

"Be careful not ta break a leg."

LOG ENTRY: 14 September, 1939. The erection of the cabling is going well. A reel was set up on each tower and at the center of the main span; then each strand was pulled across the structure by a small cable attached to a gasoline hoisting engine.

On most wire rope suspension bridges, the strands are layered together and wrapped with small wire after being given a heavy coat of lead paint. But at this bridge, the strands were placed in three layers of three strands each, spaced about 4½ inches, center to center, in both directions. The cable was not wrapped because of the added cost and because the maintenance of the open cable would not be difficult on this small of a bridge.

As soon as the three strands of the lower layer were in place, they were adjusted to the correct elevation. This adjustment was accomplished by adding steel shims at the socket at either end of the strand. The cable was first clamped at the center of the tower; then, with the normal shims in place, at both ends of the strand. Four simultaneous readings were taken: the temperature, the sag or elevation of the strand at the center of the span, and a reading at each tower as to the motion of the tower from a plumb position. Then, from charts that had been made up previously, the corrections were made by adding shims to vary the lengths of the strands. The ratio of the change in length to the change in elevation was small in the main span, being approximately 1.82, but was larger in the side spans, being approximately 6.64. Subsequent strands will be adjusted by giving them the proper clearance above the lower strands.

CHAPTER 30

OLD FISH, NEW FISH

Because of Holly, Buck came to the realization that he had to start thinking about a life beyond the ferry. Her diving into the mosquito-riddled brush above the landing, trying to watch over him like some sort of duty-bound guardian angel, was a harsh wake-up call. His hunch had been spot-on: she was worried about him. Peeking around the big maple, her skin crawling with mosquitoes, she possessed a level of devotion and concern he hadn't known she was capable of. Oh, would Ida have given him hell for putting Holly through this!

Buck felt guilty for not telling August and Belle about her visits to the landing. They would throw a fit, and justifiably so. Holly would be in the doghouse for days on end for disobeying them. But how could he stand by and see her get punished for something that was his fault?

The solace he allowed himself for not telling them was this: she clearly did not want him to see her, so she stayed well back from the high, steep bank. And without her knowing it, he always watched her closely out of the corner of his eye. He'd even gone so far as to coil a considerable length of rope in the bottom of the steer boat. He'd tied one end of it to a patched, partially inflated truck inner tube he'd gotten from Welch.

"Whaddaya need it for?" Welch had asked, handing it over, not accustomed to Shyrock asking him for anything.

"Mind your own business" was his blunt answer.

The way Buck saw it, when he was departing from the Illinois bank, Holly usually watched him for a short time before disappearing back into the thicket, always before she was out of reach of the rope. From the Indiana side, where it was too far for the rope to reach—well, this was the part that troubled him. It would be ridiculous to think he could jump in and swim to save her. But deep down, he still believed the river (although it seemed to have closed itself off from him) had consideration enough for Buck Shyrock not to take his beloved granddaughter. No one else would believe it; August and Belle wouldn't believe it, but he believed it. He did.

Trying to imagine life beyond the ferry was another matter entirely. It was like peering into the pitch-black night beyond the reach of the steer boat's headlamp, except it was a massive and mysterious lake or ocean that he was crossing and not the familiar Wabash. He had no more idea what was out there than the man in the moon. But try he must. He had to stop thinking of himself.

Seeing the mosquito bites covering Holly at Vivian's birthday party and her new secretive way of behaving around him, he realized she was suffering on his behalf. It also helped him recognize, for the first time, what he was probably putting Belle and August through. Fool that he was, he had stubbornly believed that telling them not to worry was enough—that he could take care of himself. From now on, regardless of the darkness beyond the headlamp, Holly and the others were not going to suffer on his account. No sir, they weren't.

He started by watching those who came and went on his ferry, observing them more closely and considering what their lives must be like beyond the banks of the Wabash. If he didn't know a man and what he did to make a living, he asked. If he knew the passenger, he asked him about his work. How was it going? What was he up to today?

Those who were regulars on the ferry were taken aback by his new inquisitiveness. They were accustomed to the old, gruff ferryman who looked out on the river with a somewhat superior air of aloofness, like a lord might gaze over his domain. The old Shyrock had asked no questions, wanted nothing from anyone, and, if asked a question, gave only enough of an answer to provide the minimum information required. The new Shyrock still attached little or no value to words, but he saw that words were essential to attain his goal.

Although wary at first, those who knew him gradually relaxed and enjoyed telling him of their lives—the details of their daily work that he so clearly wanted to know about.

Buck showed a special interest in Frank Weber's job at the feed mill. The burly Weber spent much of his time guiding farmers in their grain trucks onto the iron-pipe grates at the dumping station between the tall grain silos. Then he hit the lift switch that raised the truck's front wheels so the grain poured out the back and into the slotted opening in the floor. Another switch started the grain up the hiker to the top of the storage silos. Loading and unloading—he had done it his whole life. Had to be a sight easier than ferrying—something he could do, although he would miss the river.

He briefly considered becoming a mussel fisherman, but when he cornered Harry Hatch next to the ferry landing, where he kept his boat, the crusty old fisherman reminded him that musseling wasn't what it used to be in the old days. In the end, the take wasn't worth the effort. Harry blamed the decline in musseling on the young fools who, over the years hadn't wanted to bother with taking the smaller, worthless mussels off the hooks, so they threw them into the trees. "Goddamn short-sighted imbeciles," Harry said with disgust, launching a trail of tobacco juice into the river.

Shyrock already knew what came next, but he listened as Harry told him how net fishing wasn't what it used to be either. As the river got murkier from the increased farming along its banks, the game fish were in decline and the junk fish were taking over. Harry said channel cat and buffalo carp weren't worth the sweat of his brow. "Goddamn bottom-feeders. Taste like mud is all." They brought hardly anything at the fish market he ran out of a shed next to his house, just the other side of where the bridge was coming in. "Some of the younger 'uns sell 'em outta the back o' their truck over in Terrie Hut," he said. "But I can't be bothered—even if I could afford the fuel to get all the way over there an' back."

The only reason he kept doing it was out of habit, he supposed. He wouldn't know what else to do with himself if not for his early-morning forays up and down the river. "I reckon I'd dry up and die like one o' them cast-off mussels," he said, swiping with the side of his rough hand at the brown juice trickling down the corners of his mouth and into his white whiskers.

In Harry's faded eyes and sun-wrinkled face, Shyrock saw a bit of himself. Brought up short by events out of his control. The old fish pushed out by the new. But like Harry Hatch, Shyrock wouldn't give up. Not yet. He had to show the others that he wasn't done for.

CHAPTER 31

DEAL

Holly stomped and slapped and waved her arms, but nothing could discourage the mosquitoes. Her mother had asked her about the bites, and she had shrugged and told her that all she did was walk to the store and back. "Hmmm, the store, huh?" her mother said, rubbing calamine lotion into the flaming red bumps on her skin. "They must lie in wait for you. The best meal in town. Holly's Diner."

Her granddad was over at the other landing, loading a truck onto the ferry that carried a bunch of noisy pigs. They made an awful racket, clacking their hooves on the wooden truck bed and slamming repeatedly against the lumber stock racks until it sounded as if they would break clean through, and all the while squealing like they were being slaughtered right there on board the ferry.

Halfway across the river, with the pigs rampaging beside him, a movement near the old maple caught Buck's attention. He saw an elbow jut to the side and then a shock of wavy black hair, like a shred of bark had pulled loose from the tree and was fluttering in the breeze.

"Well, shit," he muttered. In his stubborn determination not to get her in trouble, he had taken chances—awful chances, he now realized. He'd been so distracted loading the truck just now, half expecting the hogs to bust open the racks, he hadn't been as vigilant as he should have been in keeping an eye on the tree. No more. He had to talk to her. Just then, she peeked around the tree and then quickly jerked her head back out of sight.

Holly knew she was caught. Her Gramps kept his eye fixed on her hiding place until it was time to land the ferry. At a loss as to what to do next, she plopped onto the ground under the tree and sat there, trying not to cry. She was in real trouble. Gramps would tell her mom and dad, and no telling what would happen then. She thought of running away from home and tried to imagine how that would go. Just thinking of it made her feel empty inside.

The truck ground its way up the steep ferry landing, its load of hogs still screaming like something out of a nightmare. After it turned left on Main Street and the pigs' ruckus was beginning to fade, her granddad called out to her.

"Holly!" he yelled. "Hey! Holly!"

She pulled her knees up tight against her chest, trying to make herself smaller. The mosquitoes buzzed all around her, and one flew into her ear, but she didn't move. Maybe he would think she had already run off.

"Holly, come down here. I know you're up there," he said sternly.

She hesitated but then answered in a small voice, "I don't want to." She dug furiously at the whining mosquito that had taken up residence in her ear.

"I'm not mad at ya," he said. "Now come on down. Please, Holly."

"You're gonna tell my mom and dad."

"We'll talk 'bout that."

He met her at the top of the landing. She ducked out of the brush, her hair full of twigs. Mosquitoes buzzed around her, delirious from the proximity of her warm blood. "I've got a 'skeeter caught in my ear," she whined, waving her soiled hand beside her head.

Buck rested his hand on her shoulder. "Stand still," he said. He put his mouth up to her ear and quickly sucked in air. When he felt the tiny insect land on his tongue, he turned and spat it out. "There ya go, sweetheart. Better?"

Buck watched her expression soften as she realized that the buzzing in her ear had stopped. But then her face worked itself into another kind of torture. "I'm in bad trouble," she moaned.

"Yeah, ya sure oughta be," he said, "don'tcha think?"

Holly nodded her head dubiously, not wanting to agree but seeing no other way out.

"Haven't your momma and daddy told ya to keep away from the river?"

She looked down at her granddad's rubber boots. There was a crack beginning to open up in one of the toes. "Yeah," she said.

"Why is that, ya think?"

"They're afraid I'll fall in and drown."

"'At's right. An' well ya could." Shyrock gazed at his granddaughter's thick black wavy hair and her sweet round face, flushed from being in the close confines of the underbrush. Suddenly, he remembered Ida as a schoolgirl. *Mercy, some things never do change.*

"Where ya s'posed ta be?"

"At the grocery."

"Well, it won't hurt if ya come inta Gramps's house for a wee bit and get a drink o' water. You look like you could use it."

"No, I better get goin'."

"It's okay. Ya can tell your mother you stopped ta see Gramps, and he offered ya a drink o' water. No harm in that, is there?"

"No, I guess not."

Once inside the house, Buck pulled out a chair from the table and told her to sit down. "Gramps has the best well water around," he bragged.

He pumped fresh water into a white enamel bucket and, using the dipper, splashed some into a glass for Holly. He crossed the room and handed it to her. Then he stood over her and waited as she lifted the glass to her mouth. "Whaddaya think, Lol?" he asked. "Pretty good, huh?"

To Holly, it was cold and satisfying, and she drank it down without lowering the glass, but it tasted the same as any other water.

He grabbed it from her hand, crossed the kitchen, and refilled it. Setting it in front of her, he settled himself into the chair next to her. "Oh, Buck," he complained, his knees feeling stiff.

Holly drew a line through the beads of water on the outside of her glass, top to bottom. Then she leaned forward and licked the glass with her tongue. She was relieved to be out of the itchy brush, away from the mosquitoes, and she couldn't remember ever having her grandfather all to herself before, especially not at his house.

Buck watched his granddaughter, waiting for the question he knew was coming. She had a flattened mosquito on her forehead, two with blood around them on her arm. He reached over and gently brushed them off, his rough hand scuffing like sandpaper against her soft skin. After that, he began plucking the twigs out of her hair. She smiled at him and started another line with the point of her tongue. She stopped halfway up the glass. "Are you going to tell?" she said, looking at him now.

"I prob'ly oughta, don't ya reckon?"

"Yeah, prob'ly." She lifted the glass and took a small sip. "I wasn't doin' it out of meanness, Gramps. Just so you know."

"Why were ya doin' it, then? When ya knew it was forbidden?"

She sat quietly, looking at the glass of water. By the troubled scowl marking her face, he knew she was struggling with a decision—wanting to tell him something but unable to decide if she should. And then, her face closed up and she said, "You won't understand."

"I won't understand, or I won't believe ya? Which one?"

"Both."

"Lol, whether or not I'll understand I can't say. But I'll always believe ya. Always."

"I'm scared," she said suddenly, searching his eyes to see his reaction and wondering whether she should have gone ahead and said it.

"Oh, it's no fun bein' scared. I been scared before."

Holly looked at him, surprised. "You?" she said.

He nodded his head and made a "puh" sound with his lips. "Plenty o' times."

"Like when?"

Buck hesitated. He thought of the first time he'd heard the river speak to him. He'd been a little older than Holly. Standing at the end of the landing, he'd almost fallen into the water—that's how startled he'd been. He had never told anyone, not even Ida. He waited a beat, two beats, and blurted it out. "What would ya say if I told you the river talked to me?" *Used to, anyway,* he thought to himself.

"Well, I'd say, doesn't it talk to everyone?"

This, he didn't expect. She looked right back at him, her eyes serious. "Nah, I don't reckon it does. But it talks to *you*?"

"Yep," she said, matter-of-factly.

"What does it say?"

"Stuff." Holly shook her head. "You first."

Buck looked at the ceiling. "It doesn't so much say things," he said, hesitating, trying to get the words right. "It doesn't say things out loud, ya know? It speaks to my head, my mind, is more like it, directly into my head. It's not words. It's . . . feelings, more like. Enough that I know what it means. What it intends for me to understand."

Holly was nodding her head. "It doesn't have to say words. You just know."

"And what do you know?"

"I know that you're going to be okay. The river told me. Just today when you were over across the river."

"Why wouldn't Gramps be okay, sweetie?"

It popped out of her mouth before she even knew she was going to say it. "I saw you die!" Her face knotted up into an ugly grimace, and she began to cry.

Buck reached and took her hand in his. "Lol, you musta had a bad dream. Gramps ain't gonna die. Not for a long time. Just a bad dream is all it was."

"But I wasn't sleepin' . . . I was awake . . . at the grocery," she sobbed.

This stopped him for a moment, and he looked at her, surprised.

"I was awake, and I saw you die," she bawled.

"Aw, come here," he said, pushing his chair back from the table and opening his arms to her.

She climbed onto his lap and he wrapped his arms around her. "That doesn't mean it's gonna come true. Not at all." Buck spoke soothingly to her and rubbed his big, flat hand up and down her back. She felt so fragile. He could have counted each of her little ribs if he wanted to. His heart broke open and flooded his chest with love and compassion for this amazing little girl. His own flesh and blood. Protecting her from all hurt and harm suddenly seemed to him the most important thing he could ever do with his life.

"Gramps'll be okay, sweetheart," he whispered.

Her sobs had subsided now to sniffles. He leaned forward and pulled a red bandana out of his hip pocket and held it to her nose. "Blow," he said.

It was the first time he had ever held a handkerchief to a child's nose. When she blew out, he felt the warm air from her nostrils against his fingertips. What a strangely beautiful thing it was. This is what Ida felt every time she held a handkerchief to little Auggie's nose when he was a small child—what she'd known she was missing out on when their baby had died. "You're a very special little girl. You know that?"

"What about the ferry? What about the bridge?"

"Is that what you're worried about? Goodness gracious, I intend ta find somethin' to keep myself busy," he said.

"And I intend ta spend more time with my gran'daughters, for one. How's that sound?"

"Good," she said in a small voice.

Buck took her chin in his hand and raised her head so she was looking at him. "'Bout you bein' at the river. That's to be our secret, on one condition. You know what that is?"

"That I promise to never do it again."

"Not ever. If you want to see Gramps, you come straight to the house, or you wait for me at the top of the landing. Deal?"

Holly nodded her head. "Deal."

"And no more worryin'."

She nodded again. "Deal."

Buck looked down at Rebel, who sat with her head on his knee next to Holly's leg. She gazed up at the two of them, her sad eyes moving from one to the other. "Rebel, how 'bout it, girl? Deal?"

The hound raised her head and bayed.

"I think that means yes," Buck laughed. "And she always keeps secrets."

Holly began laughing, too, and patted Rebel on the head. Rebel licked her hand.

"Kisses," Shyrock said. "She's kissin' you."

"I love you, too, ol' Rebel," Holly said, and bent down and planted a big kiss on the dog's snout.

Shyrock hugged her and set her on the floor. "You better skedaddle. Your momma will be worried."

Holly leaned in and gave him a quick peck on the cheek and then ran out the door. "Bye, Rebel," she called, the screen door slamming behind her.

After she was gone, Buck stayed in the same spot, watching the leaf shadows from the black walnut tree flicker about on the kitchen wall, like winged faeries dancing in a patch of sunlight.

She'd seen him die. Die.

"Stephen Shyrock, you sorry son of a gun," he said out loud.

Rebel lowered her ears as if she was the one being scolded.

"I don't know how you put up with me, girl," he said, shaking his head with self-loathing. "A man that'd scare his own grandbaby ain't much of a man, is he?"

A car horn tooted from over in Indiana, tooted a second time and then, after a pause, again. While Buck pulled on his boots, the hound sauntered over to the screen door and pushed it open with her nose. Standing on the porch, looking across the breeze-dappled river in the direction of the waiting car, she barked accusingly, as if to say, "What's your big hurry?"

CHAPTER 32

NAKED MOON

The moon slid behind a bank of clouds, as silent and smooth as a coin slipping into an empty pocket. Will Turner took advantage of the moment to step quickly out from behind the shadow of the Ford garage. Just as quickly, he jumped back in when he heard Shyrock's door creak open and the hound's nails tap across the porch floor. Turner flattened himself, face first, against the musty-smelling concrete wall as the dog ran down the porch steps. Cursing the animal under his breath, he watched it take a leak in the center of the yard, turn to smell its own puddle, and then make its usual circuit around the lawn's perimeter, sniffing at each corner, stopping to circle the outhouse, nose to the ground.

When the moon popped out from behind the clouds, suddenly flooding the treeless backyard in harsh white light, Will crowded closer to the wall, and the half-pint bottle chinked in his pocket. The dog stopped in its tracks and looked directly at him. Will froze, holding his breath. Nose up, the dog sniffed at the air. Waiting for it to bark, Will pictured his escape path through the narrow alley between the garage and the post office that opened onto Main Street. But the hound lowered its head, smelled the ground one last time, and then turned and beat a path straight to the porch.

Nails clicked on wood, and after a few moments, Turner heard the door open and close again. All grew quiet, inside and outside the house. One light shone from the kitchen window.

Turner waited a couple of minutes and then relaxed, leaning back against the cool wall. He lit a cigarette and took a swig from his whiskey bottle. The old man would not be coming out again unless a nighttime traveler beckoned him to the river. Over the past several weeks of surveilling the house, it had become clear that Shyrock didn't use the outdoor privy after seven o'clock.

Turner wasn't accustomed to all this watching and waiting, and it made him fidgety. He had failed at all of the things in his life that required patience: earning passing grades at school, getting paid after a job was finished. Even as a child, he was never able to sit quietly long enough to receive a promised piece of candy. Instead, he fussed, red-faced, demanding it *now,* until what he got in place of the candy was a thrashing. If there was something he wanted, he would take the quickest, most direct course to that end. And anyone who stood in his way was added, posthaste, to his substantial list of enemies.

This time it was different. Since the night he had been booted off the ferry, Will had been plotting his revenge against Shyrock. First, the old bastard had gotten him thrown in jail for helping himself to a little bit of gas out of that big old tank. Hardly even enough to notice. Then he'd had the balls to kick him off the ferry when it was Shyrock's hound that had attacked *him.* Turner could easily take his revenge anytime he wanted. But he waited, delighting in his surveillance of Shyrock's house. The lurking about unseen was as much a part of the payback as the act of vengeance itself.

Some nights, he skulked about the property almost until daylight, noting when Shyrock turned out his light for bed, when and how many times he let the dog out to piss, the part of the yard where the dog squatted to take a shit, its patterns of movement. Shyrock kept a predictable and steady routine. The light went on in the bedroom and out in the kitchen at nearly the same time every night. Not long after, the house went dark.

The old man had no idea who the hell he was dealing with. He would be sorry he'd ever fucked with Will Turner. Sorrier than all hell.

LOG ENTRY: 22 September, 1939. When all the strands in the main cable had been placed and adjusted, the suspender cables were clamped to the main cable at the points already marked and then connected to the stiffening girders, which were on falsework one foot above their final dead-load position. Jacks for lowering the girders were placed at the towers, the girder ends, and on intermediate bents in each span. Keeping the lashing that held the girders longitudinally at the Illinois or west abutment taut at all times, the south girder over its entire length was first lowered ½ inch at a time, a total of 2 inches The north girder was then similarly lowered a total of 4 inches, and progressive lowering of both girders was carried out in the same way for the total 12 inches at the towers and girder ends. Pulling by use of turnbuckles was required to lower the girders at the towers and girder ends, though the pulling at the towers was slight. Once in dead-load position, the timber falsework was removed and the cables took up the load.

At this critical juncture, a cheer went up among the construction crew. The old men watching from the Illinois bank followed suit. A memorable moment for all involved. The bridge now "stands" on its own!

CHAPTER 33
EVERYTHING RETURNS

Unable to sleep, Shyrock had just lately begun sitting by the river at night. Although he felt foolish doing it, he now sat at the edge of the ferry landing, his boots and curled socks beside him, soaking his pale bare feet in the slow, lazy current. Rebel lay on the concrete behind him, her nose in the air, sniffing. In Millerville, there was an old saying: *Those who get their feet muddy in the Wabash will always return to it*. Well, he had never left it, but turning the adage over in his mind, Shyrock thought of one of the many things the river had taught him: everything returns. If this was indeed true, that everything returns, then when would the voice of the Wabash return to him?

As he'd often done since the stranger on the Indiana bank started his world turning upside down, Buck turned his ear to the river. He felt the hulking, shadowy bridge off to his left; he didn't need eyes to be aware of its presence. Beneath him, the current lapped at the concrete. Next to him, the ferry creaked at its ropes. These, anyone could hear. He needed more. He couldn't help but believe that the river had something it wanted to say to him, something he should know, the one thing that would save him from the mess he was in. He felt himself growing more desperate the longer the river remained silent to his ears. Is this the way it would be? What if it never returned for him? What then?

From deep in the Illinois woods that grew right up to the bank downriver from where Shyrock sat brooding came the hoot of an owl. Normally, the call of anything wild cheered Shyrock, but tonight, in his present state of mind, he received it as an omen. He had never believed the superstitious fools who claimed an owl's call portended death; hardly a night went by that he didn't hear an owl's call echoing somewhere along the river. But on this particular night, the *whoo, whoo, whooooo* sent a shiver up his spine. Suddenly feeling cold, noticing for the first time the autumn chill in the air, he lifted his feet out of the water and dried them on his socks.

As he prepared to return to the house, the owl flew closer and then landed in the giant maple whose limbs reached over the landing above him. It sat high in the tree, directly over his head. As it resumed its call, it was so close he could hear the maneuverings of its vocal chords with each new utterance it made, more like the internal workings of a clock—levers rising and falling, cogs turning—than a force of nature.

Shyrock clambered to his feet. "Hey!" he hollered at the hooting owl, waving his arms. "Go on! Git!"

From its limb, the owl gazed down at him with its all-seeing, night-lit eyes. It spun its feathery head and pointed ears in that impossible circle, first one way and then the other, as if it were mocking him.

Finally, when Shyrock couldn't take it anymore, he bellowed as loud as he could, "I said *git*!"

The big bird dropped leisurely off the limb and soundlessly spread its long, tapered wings, turning on its own axis to head back the way it had come.

Feeling spooked, even while telling himself it was a lot of hooey, Shyrock finished pulling on his boots and hightailed it as fast as his old legs would take him up the length of the ferry landing.

Before going in the house, he glanced once more at the tree to see if the owl had returned. Only then did he notice that Rebel wasn't by his side.

CHAPTER 34

ARTFUL DODGER

It was more out of bewilderment than any genuine desire for animal companionship that John Welch got himself a dog.

His puzzlement arose from a question he had asked himself more and more as he tried to be a support for Shyrock. Really, what did they have in common when it came right down to it? He was a farmer and Buck Shyrock a ferryman. He had spent most of his days bouncing over hard dry land, while Shyrock shimmied over a rush of water and whatever buoyancy it afforded. John Welch valued the written word and was a voracious reader of books as well as newspapers. And he enjoyed talking to people, like he had enjoyed conversing with Floyd Bailey over breakfast. Shyrock had little use for words, regardless of the form in which they were presented. While Shyrock had family, he himself was alone, if not comfortably then at least tolerably. True, they had both lost their wives within the past five years, but that topic was still too tender to touch in the harsh light of day when there was work to be done. Once touched, there was no telling where it would lead them. Neither much liked unchartered territory, so they shied away from it. If there was any mention of their wives, they both spoke in clouded terms, as if their respective mates waited at home in some sort of suspended animation, not living exactly, but not totally gone either.

Plainly said, they irritated one another. Argument was their medium. Anything else was like a foreign language—snippets and single words spoken awkwardly, hinting only briefly at some deeper feeling and then quickly deserted for snipes and swipes and tongue-lashings. They had often gone days without seeing one another, and if not for the necessity of the ferry, it would no doubt have lapsed into weeks, if not months. There was not what you would call pleasure in their encounters.

What bound them together more than anything was the passage of years in the same locale—seeing changes and remembering how it once was when very few others did. Out of this parallel journey a friendship had rattled along, like an old, nearly worn-out jalopy bouncing over a washboard road, holding itself together against all odds.

Friendship. Whatever that word meant, wherever it left them, Welch was still at a loss. From this stance, a foot in, a foot out, how was he to help? Shyrock was clearly adrift. If not an anchor, he at least needed a rope.

So John Welch got himself a dog. Shyrock loved his dog; this much was clear. If nothing else, maybe they could swap stories about their dogs. *My dog did this; my dog did that* sort of thing.

Besides, Welch had a healthy dose of plain orneriness that came into the mix—Shyrock didn't believe he would get a dog.

$$\approx \approx \approx$$

As Shyrock had suggested, Welch had asked around until someone told him where there was a new litter of pups. It turned out there were beagle pups at a farm just across a couple of fields from his own. When Welch went to have a look, still not sure it was for the best that he get a dog, this little flop-eared varmint, not much bigger than a rat, spotted him out of the corner of his eye, tore himself loose from the wriggling mound of black and white and penny-colored fur, and wobbled over to him. With a hop and some scrabbling of paws, the pup sprawled over the top of Welch's boot and grunted, same as to say, "Ready when you are." And that was that.

Heading straight over to Shyrock's house, the pup dozing on his lap, Welch could already picture it in his mind. "Well, I've gone and done it," he would say. "Done what?" Shyrock would ask. But that's not the way it went. The way it did go was as far from what he'd imagined as was earthly possible.

It was still early morning when he turned off Main Street at the Ford garage. Drawing closer, he spotted the line of vehicles on the ferry landing: Lee Miller's faded red International tractor by itself at the front; a car; and then a pickup truck, too clean and new-looking to be from around here. They were all empty, their occupants nowhere in sight. The hair on Welch's neck stood up.

He parked to the left of the landing, left the pup in the truck, and hurried across the yard.

Three men were on the porch. Welch recognized Lee Miller sitting on the porch rail, a white tobacco pouch hanging from his teeth as he rolled a cigarette with his thick, callused hands.

"Lee, what's goin' on? What's wrong?"

"He ain't comin' out," Miller said. Looking up from his cigarette, he glanced at the door. "See him sittin' there at the table, but he won't budge. Can't even get him to look up."

"Won't come out?" Welch echoed, making sure he'd heard it correctly.

"Nope," Miller said, "he won't."

The two strangers stepped back as though they'd stumbled into a place where they had no business being and didn't want to be blamed for whatever was going on. For no other reason than the stupid looks on their faces, Welch had an urge to push them backward over the rail and to slap the cigarette out of Miller's calm hands before launching him over, too. Behind them, beyond the porch and the leafy brush that had started turning color since Welch had been here last, the Wabash glimmered like cooling silver. Welch strode to the door and opened it.

As Miller had said, Buck was sitting quietly, staring at his hands, which rested side by side on the table in front of him.

"Shyrock? What's . . . happened?" Welch said uncertainly, the words choosing themselves.

Shyrock looked up, his eyes all out of whack. He raised his right hand and swiped it awkwardly across his mouth. Welch heard the scratch of whiskers and the scrape of air across dry lips and tongue.

"Killed m'dog," he rasped, finally, as if it took all the energy he could muster.

"Aw, no. Rebel?" Welch said. "Christ."

He crossed the kitchen to the pump to get Shyrock a glass of water. The way he drooped, he looked to have been sitting there all night.

"How?"

"Glass."

"Aw, God." Welch could surmise the rest himself. Ground glass mixed in with minced-up meat. Dog gobbles it so quickly, without stopping to chew, the inner ruin is well on its way before the animal even takes a breath. The oldest trick in the book, among heartless, vile cowards the world over.

Welch set the water glass in front of Shyrock.

"I am truly sorry," he said, laying his hand on Buck's shoulder. "Don't you worry. I'll take care o' things. You just sit there. Drink some water."

"B-bury her?" Shyrock stammered. "Hate askin' it."

"Sure—on the farm okay?"

Shyrock nodded slowly, like his head was a burden too heavy to hold up for very long. "That . . ." he faltered and then took a long, ragged breath. "That'd be all right."

Welch moved into action. He threw his truck keys at Lee Miller and told him to go find August. Welch would move Lee's tractor out of the way and take the others across on the ferry.

"Watch out for the pup. He's new to this world. His name is Dodger." He had just come up with it on the spur of the moment, as in the Artful Dodger from *Oliver Twist*. All things considered, a good name for a dog, he reckoned.

After a slow, laborious takeoff and an abrupt landing, Welch returned to the Illinois launch. He moored the ferry the best he could, playing Shyrock's ritual over in his mind, wishing he'd paid better attention. Then he traversed the yard until he found the drag marks. Not yet ready for the harsh reality of where the marks led, he traced them backward to the outhouse. Up close against the south wall, he saw where the dog had fallen. There were blood smears on the weathered siding, about head high for the dog, where Rebel must have faltered before collapsing. Welch followed the trail of blood around the back (*Fares Took Here . . . Holy Christ, what Shyrock has to put up with*), the dried brownish maroon drops diminishing and finally petering out when he'd reached the privy's opposite wall. There, an imperfect round grease mark in the thin grass and dirt. As he bent closer, a few tiny shards of glass that had fallen out of the meat when the dog gobbled it up.

Pissant—the word popped into his head. He recalled the conversation with Shyrock concerning the stolen gas and the angry threats he'd heard repeated around town. Will Turner, that worthless coward. Welch wanted to go straight over and stave in his head with a two-by-four that was in the back of his truck. He was almost relieved when he remembered Miller had taken the truck to find August.

Now, walking back the other way, the elongated scrapes in the dirt, the flattened grass, gave testament to how Shyrock had pulled his beloved dog across the yard, tugging again and again, until he reached the north side of the house, where she now lay. Mercy. Lolling, swollen tongue; misshapen, bloodied mouth; eyes empty, staring. Shyrock had gone in and grabbed a rug off the floor to lay the dog on—a rag rug, one of several that Ida had made. There was one in Welch's house that Ida had given to Edna. He'd almost forgotten that Ida and his wife had been childhood friends, not seeing one another so much in their adult years since neither of them drove. *I should have done more to bring them together*, he thought now, much too late.

Shyrock had laid Rebel out on the rug and dragged her over here where she would be out of sight, hidden from the public eye. Welch was grateful that there had been a hard freeze so there were no flies. He nudged her haunch with the toe of his boot. Deader 'n a goldang doornail. The lump in his throat grew larger.

Over on the Indiana side, the hammering of a tractor scaling the levee roused him from whatever stink hole he had descended into, mulling over living and dying and decay. *Humans are no different from the rest,* he realized, *doing what's required, with little thought and, most of the time, even less feeling, eating whatever shit is fed us.*

What business did he have getting a dog? His old heart had turned almost to charcoal. He would take it back this morning and say it was a mistake, a hasty decision, and that he was very sorry for the inconvenience.

But first, he had to deliver that tractor from over across the way and then wait for Lee to come back with his truck and for August to take over operating the ferry.

Leaving Rebel where she lay, Welch rounded the house on the side facing the river. Scuffing across the thin brown grass, past the porch, he barely resisted the urge to kick one of the stone floor supports as he muttered under his breath, "I'm goin'! I'm goin'! Jus' drink the goddamned water, Shyrock!"

CHAPTER 35

POOR GOD

"Really, though, Belle, it *was* only a dog. I don't know why you're so upset."

"Rebel was *his* dog. She was like family to him," Belle said, trying to be patient but feeling annoyed at having to explain to her husband something most people would find obvious. "She was special. To him, she was special."

"We're his family. A dog is a pet."

Belle shook her head and puffed out her cheeks in exasperation. This pigheadedness between son and father, like a contest to see who could be the most implacable in not seeing the other's point of view, was wearing on her. Pigheaded was one thing; insensitivity was another.

"Did you know he went right back to work after Elizabeth died? Pert' near left Mom on her own, to sink or swim." Slowing the truck to make the final turn, he glanced at her to gauge her reaction.

"How do you even know that? You weren't born yet."

"I was told," August said. He kicked in the clutch and downshifted.

Belle's upper torso jerked forward. "You were told," she said. "Okay, granted, some people show their grief differently than others."

"They sure must," August answered.

Rolling to a stop next to the house, they sat peering across the river where the willow trees were almost done shedding their leaves. The remaining ones hung, lackluster at the ends of the sagging limbs, as if they'd seen too much sun, too much wind, too much everything. They looked ready to be done with it. Welch, having unloaded Lee Miller and his tractor, was just leaving from the other bank.

Belle spoke first. "I suppose it doesn't take a sympathetic heart to steer the ferry," she said, without turning to look at him.

August jerked up on the door handle and nudged the door with his shoulder. "I'll look in on him before I go out."

"Keep your opinion to yourself, please."

August rolled his eyes. "Of course," he said.

$$\approx \approx \approx$$

"Hi, Dad." August hesitated in the doorway, letting his eyes adjust to the inner gloom of the house. He could just make out his father's bent image, the faded blue sleeve of his work shirt. "Can I come in?"

Shyrock coughed and tried to speak but only managed a croaking sound. He put his hand to his throat and waved August in. He then pushed his hand over the surface of the table to a glass setting in front of him and drank it down in one draught.

August entered the house with Belle close behind him.

"August," Buck finally managed to say. "Belle." He didn't look at either of them.

"A rough start to your day," August said.

"Last night, it was."

Belle stepped around August and laid her hands on the big, stooped shoulders. "Is that when you found her, Dad? Is that when you found Rebel?"

Buck reached with his left hand across his own chest and grabbed hold of Belle's fingers.

"What some people are capable of," Belle said.

"Dad, I'll go relieve Welch. Don't want an inexperienced hand cracking it in two against the cement," August said, trying to make a joke.

"Don't matter if he does. Let him."

Belle's eyes jumped to August. She was about to say, *Of course it does, Dad. That's your ferry we're talking about.* But she found herself agreeing with him. Was it really his concern anymore whether or not people got across the river? One of their own number was so wicked and cruel as to kill his beloved dog in a torturous and inhumane way. Let them swim until their bridge was done.

August touched her on the arm. "I'm goin'," he said.

Keeping a tight hold on Buck's hand, Belle dropped into the chair next to him. Buck looked at her for the first time. He started to say something, but his throat made only a croaking noise, immediately closing up on him. Belle jumped up and carried the empty glass over to the counter. Working the pump, she splashed water into it until it overflowed and then quickly crossed the kitchen and set it in front of him again.

He drank some down. A rivulet escaped out the side of his mouth and trickled down his white-stubbled neck. Buck swiped at it with the back of his hand and set the glass down on the wood. Out of breath, he drew in just enough air so he could speak. "He same as told me he was gonna do it, but I didn't take him seriously enough."

"You mean hurt Rebel? Who told you?"

"That Turner boy. Drunk as I've ever seen a man. Told me I'd be sorry after she knocked him on his ass-end for threat'nin' me. I ordered him offa the boat. Thought that'd be the end of it. I shoulda knowed better. He's bad."

"Will Turner? I knew he stole your gas, but you didn't say anything about a threat."

"My own stupidity to just forget about it." He thought again of what John Welch had told him: "Word around town is he means you harm. *And the dog.*"

They both heard an unsettling screech, the sound of the ferry's apron scraping heavily over concrete. Welch apparently hadn't raised it quite enough to clear the landing's sharp incline. Belle waited for Buck to react. Meeting her eyes, he only shrugged.

"Well, Dad, what do we do now?" Belle asked.

Shyrock looked at her, the dullness of his eyes showing little interest in thinking up an answer to her question. But he did speak. "Much as I don't care if I ever get out of this chair, I'm gonna go watch my boy run the ferry. Never thought I'd see it again. Likely won't after this."

≈ ≈ ≈

He still had it in him. For all his resistance, August had picked up ferrying like he'd been born with a tiller in his hand. Standing there on the high bank, watching his son, Buck recalled that was why he'd been so angry and disappointed when August had walked away from his apprenticeship. He *had* it, just as Buck's father had had it. He made it look effortless—the way he held the rope and whipped it around the anchor post with ease and perfect accuracy, his back straight, his arms doing the work. The air of authority he displayed in getting the vehicles on and off the ferry. The smooth, efficient way he got the ferry moving, and the velvety touch with which he landed it on the opposite side. And most important of all, his way with the river. He was a natural. Like he understood it, and it understood him. Like he was born to it. Like it was in his blood.

In his blood. His birthright.

≈ ≈ ≈

Belle stayed back on the porch, not wanting to disturb Buck's reverie. She watched him at the edge of the yard, where it ended and the steep riverbank took over. The toes of his worn gum boots pressed right up to the thick weeds and stringy, knotted vines. He looked older now; she could see it so plainly. August had always called him "the old man," but now he *was* old—his shoulders stooped, something of his leathery toughness gone. There was a new softness to him. The words *the golden years* came to mind and suddenly, watching him, she knew exactly what the words meant. The past and the present, together, there in plain view, giving him a burnished look, like an autumn landscape at sunset; not done but winding down toward its conclusion.

Tranquil was how he looked now, as if all the challenges, the miserable losses, the dismal failures, and the fine glowing moments of his life had merged together. The once discordant fragments turned, returning to this one place, where he stood looking over the river, his life nearly complete. Because of the old ones like him, Belle thought, the path ahead had been made more passable, less strewn with hazards, less treacherous.

Oh, he was something, August's father, their daughters' grandfather. God threw away the mold when he made him. Then again, Belle was pretty sure Dad had broken it himself, busting out before God was done. He wasn't perfect, far from it, but he was beautiful just the same.

"Made in God's image," the Good Book said. *But none of us is perfect*, she mused. *Maybe that's what we all do—impatient, raring to go, we burst out of the casting before God is done with his handiwork. Poor God. All of us imperfect souls mucking around, creating havoc with what he tried to make perfect for us but somehow, finding our way through. God seemed to put up with us, finding us beautiful just the same.*

It was due to the sight of his son on the river that the very next day, Shyrock took back the ferry's helm. The bridge was nearly done, and his days as a ferryman were numbered. He might as well see it through, meet it head on, like a man. His swan song. The cavern in his chest, left by Rebel's passing, would be there a long time. He knew from long experience that he could still move through life with his heart exposed to the sun and the rain and the blowing wind—the grit of life. Yes, he might as well get on with it.

LOG ENTRY: 13 October, 1939. The traverse floor beams have been placed, spaced 25 feet on center, framed into the side girders, alternately, over the pile bent and at the center of each span. Four 18-inch stringers between these floor beams will carry the floor, which will be concrete-filled 4½-inch, I-Beam-Lok type with a 20-foot clear roadway. Supports are being erected in the side spans, though that precaution is likely not necessary.

CHAPTER 36

THE BLUE EYE

August hadn't planned it. He'd never been a brawler, and the only time he ever used his fist—to strike another boy who'd squirted motor oil down the back of his neck—his heart wasn't in it. He'd drawn back on the punch just before contact, and the boy had laughed at him for "hitting like a girl."

But there was something about Will Turner strutting along the street, easy as you please, fag hanging from his mouth in that cocky, derisive way, exercising the rights of a regular citizen, that made August want to draw blood. He veered his pickup onto the verge directly in front of Turner, stopping him in his tracks.

As August jumped out of the pickup, his eyes quickly swept the surrounding neighborhood to see if anyone was out and watching. Surprise and fear flashed across Will's face as he glanced around for an escape route. Before he could run, August grabbed him by the collar of his jacket, spun him around, and rammed him into the side of the truck. Turner was nearly a head taller, but August was thicker and stronger, and the element of surprise worked in his favor.

"What're you *doin'*?" Turner bleated in terror.

Now that he had him in his grip, August felt his own eyes bulging, his breath coming hot and labored, like he might run out of air. *You're not very good at this, you idiot,* he thought.

"What am I doin'?" August panted, struggling to keep his voice even.

Turner caught the moment of uncertainty in his assailant's face. Quick to spot weaknesses and turn them to his own advantage, he licked his lips and protested, "Hey, you got the wrong man." He assumed a humble expression and used the sincerest tone he could manage, hoping to keep August slightly off balance and introduce doubt in his mind.

It didn't work. Up close, Turner had a smarmy mug that looked incapable of sincerity and a stranger to truth. To match it, his breath was foul from bad teeth, stale beer, and cigarettes. August slapped him hard across the face. The sharp sting in his hand made him more focused, putting all his senses on high alert.

"The hell I do," August growled, in full control now. "You've already told it all around town."

Virgil White had told August about it at the township shed the other morning before they started work. "None o' my bizness, rilly, but thought ya oughta know," he'd said. In the light of the shed's bare bulb, his wan face was a sickly yellow from a night of drinking. "That Turner boy was talkin' up at the Old York Tavern, drunker 'n two hoots in a holler. Told a feller he's the one kilt your daddy's hound. Said he had no choice. He'd already promised it to your ol' man that he'd make him sorry. Somethin' that happened on the ferry, he said. Said he always keeps a promise—like it was a goddamn point of honor." Virgil told how people up at the bar had moved away from Turner then. "Sorry fuck," someone had called him. Virgil licked his dry, cracked lips. "Opens his mouth when he oughta be keepin' it shut s'what he keeps doin'. That boy always was a damn fool. Like his daddy, I reckon."

"You threatened my dad," August said now. "You did what you said you'd do—make him sorry for kickin' you off the ferry. For havin' you thrown in jail. Kept your promise all right. You killed his dog."

"Threaten? His dawg? Who told you that? I'd never—"

August jerked his collar tight and smacked him again. "You lyin' son of a bitch!" he barked into Turner's face. "You mashed that glass into little pieces, wrapped it in meat, and put it where my dad's dog'd find it."

His ear ringing like a fire bell, Turner ran through his options. Fight back. Keep denying it. Tell him to fuck off—*yeah, I did it, and I ain't regrettin' doin' it, either.* Admitting he'd done it would land him in jail again, sure as hell. He was already at a disadvantage in the quickness and balance department if he were to fight back; his head was spinning, and he saw glaring jabs of light from the two solid cuffs to the side of his head. *So keep denyin' it, Will.* But before he could form the words of a denial in his befuddled brain, he was sprawled on his back in the street, his feet kicking at gravel. Above him, the sky was a big blue eye, open wide, unblinking, laughing down at him and his bad luck.

August knelt next to him. "You think you're such a tough guy, Turner. But anyone who'd lurk around an old man's house like a skunk, under cover of darkness, and glass his dog ain't tough. He's just a goddamn coward."

Will blinked his eyes as if not sure where to look.

"You *ever* go near my father or his house again . . ." August shook his head, as if he didn't want to contemplate, for Turner's sake, how that sentence would end. "You even *see* him, you best head the other direction fast as your legs'll carry ya. Understood?"

The blue eye laughed and kept on laughing. *Blink, goddamn you! Blink!*

Gravel and a cloud of exhaust spewed over Will as August started the engine and drove away in his truck.

LOG ENTRY: 23 October, 1939. Placing and welding of the steel grid floor has been completed in the side spans. This will be followed by concreting, and then the same process in the main span. Getting close now.

CHAPTER 37

THE OLD TIRED WIND

From Edna's chair, John Welch looked across the yard past where the garden used to be, where the earth sagged as if weary from so many years of growing his and Edna's vegetables, to the crusted mound of dirt. Scattered all around it were the rough little wood crosses that Edna had fashioned out of lattice board she'd had him filch from an abandoned and derelict farmhouse down the road a ways. Every time she found a bird lying dead somewhere around their place and occasionally under the big window where Welch now sat reading his newspapers (these she took the hardest), she buried it out there next to the vegetable garden, close in to the peonies.

"They work so hard for us," Edna had said once, her voice teary. She'd held a purple finch gently in her hand until its heart played out and it shivered against her palm; then she lifted it so he could see its eyes—black shiny beads mirroring back the light—and how its head had been wrenched to the side from its collision with the window glass. "Singing, singing, singing their little hearts out!" she cried. "What a sad place this world would be without them." *Be sad without you, too, my dear*, he remembered thinking at the time.

Welch could see which were the cardinals' graves. Edna had made the crosses taller and wider for her beloved redbirds. She'd even painted them white, though nearly all the white paint was gone now. In deference to Edna, Welch kept all the crosses standing up straight and renailed the horizontal arms back to the uprights whenever one of them worked loose. Rebel's grave would need some kind of marker. He had thought about mentioning it to Shyrock, but why trouble him just yet? If it was important to him, if he wanted it done sooner than later, he would say something.

Nonetheless, Welch rolled it over in his mind. He'd seen people nail their dog's collar to a cross. But Shyrock had never put a collar on Rebel. "She came without one, she'll stay that way," Shyrock had told him when he'd suggested it might be a good idea, to show she had an owner. "An owner?" he'd responded, as if it was the damndest fool statement he'd ever heard. "I don't own her any more 'n she owns me. Ya thinkin' I should lug a collar around on my neck, too, Welch?" As with most of his suggestions to Shyrock, that was the end of it.

Welch looked back at his *Indianapolis News* drooping in his hands. He snapped it taut and turned to the second page. The headline "Ribbon Cutting Planned for Sullivan-Millerville Bridge" jumped out at him from the middle of the page.

Although there was much work to be done, the article said, anticipation was growing over its completion. The dedication and ribbon-cutting ceremony had been slated for the sixteenth of December. A big crowd was expected. The mayor of Millerville, Harvey Ash, was quoted: "This is the biggest thing to ever come to our town. It's all people can talk about." Dignitaries, including the governors of both Indiana and Illinois, had been invited. There was a statement from the chairman of the bridge commission, touting the anticipated financial impact of the new bridge on the regional economy.

Welch folded the newspaper thoughtfully and set it on the table next to his chair. He looked out over the yard again, at all of Edna's faded crosses, at the settled earth of the old garden where now only water grass and dandelions grew, and at the sad mound of already fading dirt under which Rebel lay. The weight of all time fell heavy on his legs, pressing them down into the chair cushion until he thought he'd go clear through to the floor and, not stopping, on into the earth, where he'd sink and sink and never be found, leaving not even a trace. *I worked so hard for them* were the last fading words that Welch heard as he dropped into sleep. It was Shyrock's voice, dry and ratty as the old, tired wind.

Welch dreamed about a bridge falling. Plumes of black dust shot into the air; steel and concrete debris peppered the water below only moments before the entire bridge deck collapsed downward with a mighty, gut-wrenching *whoomp!* The twin support towers, in unison, tipped toward each other in defeat, like a boxer sagging at the knees.

CHAPTER 38

WAS IT LOVE?

Belle charged into the newspaper office. The door slammed against the inside wall, rattling the glass. Wilbur Smith sat at a desk behind the counter. Behind him was the hulking black press, always wiped clean as a new tomorrow. Its single lever jutted out the side, as big and impressive as the arm on a teamster. Wilbur looked calmly over his reading glasses at her, as if people slammed into his news agency every day. "May I help you with something?" he asked.

The sight of the printing press, its complexity, its mass, its power to produce words on paper that are seen by so many eyes, cowed her for a moment, and she stood there at a loss, feeling out of her element, almost forgetting why she was there. But then the back door opened and in walked Dorothy Smith, looking at the floor, not seeing her at first.

Belle looked back at Wilbur Smith. "I think it's too late to help with anything. The damage, I would imagine, is already done." She shook the *Gazette* that she grasped in her raised hand.

Out of the corner of her eye, she saw Dorothy look up in surprise.

"What damage would that be?" he asked, undisturbed in his demeanor—the calm, impartial newspaper man, trying to get at the facts, even if they came as an accusation aimed at him.

Belle snapped the newspaper open in front of Dorothy, straightened her spine, lifted her chin with dramatic zeal, and read from the first page. "Finally, the time has almost come for us to dismantle the oil-stained, rotting old ferry and to send its aged *El Capitan* to the retirement bench on Main Street. There he can thrill his peers with stories of old battles fought with the river, albeit adventures that will carry something of a ridiculous tone, since our new bridge will have allowed us to sound the bugle call of victory, the vanquished river knowing its place." Belle's voice rose higher and higher in volume with each word, mocking the drama of the words. She ended by throwing the newspaper on the floor and stomping her foot on it.

Wilbur Smith gave his wife a bland look, as if to say, "I told you not to publish it. Now *you* take care of the mess it's caused."

Dorothy removed her coat and brushed down its length several times with her hand. Then she turned and hung it on a hook by the back door. She patted her hair and walked confidently to the counter. "What's this?" she said, lifting her nose to give Belle a derisive look.

"*This* is about enough. You've insulted my father-in-law for the last time."

"Insulted? I've merely stated my view. My view of things as they are." Dorothy looked down her nose at Belle and said as if she was talking to a first-grader, "That's what opinion pieces do." She ended with a nasty smile and a sniff.

Belle stepped up to the counter and looked across it at Dorothy, their eyes on the same level. Dorothy's eyes widened and then narrowed again, resuming their condescending look of disapproval. There were squiggly little veins worming angrily away from the green of her irises. Belle repeated what she'd said. "You have insulted my father-in-law for the last time."

"You talk as if you think you can stop me." Dorothy sniffed again and then her nostrils flared.

"Dorothy Smith, have you always had a heart made of stone? Or have you acquired it slowly, with each new disappointment? I'm sure coming here to Millerville from Chicago must have been a shock—all of us country bumpkins, so far beneath you. What made you stay?" She looked at Wilbur Smith and smiled cruelly. "Was it love that made you stay?"

Strangely, Wilbur smiled back at her but sadly.

"Why . . . I'm sorry," Belle said, and she really meant it. She turned away from Dorothy now. Ignoring her, she looked at Wilbur. Suddenly, she liked this man. She saw the loneliness in those sad, intelligent eyes, that melancholy smile. He had been a part of the town, having been born and raised here. But his leaving to go to university, living in Chicago, being formally educated, and marrying Dorothy had driven a wedge between him and the rest of the townspeople. She'd heard the talk. *Stuck up. Thinks he's better than the rest of us.*

"I'm *asking* you to not be cruel to my father-in-law," Belle said to him. "That's all I'm asking. He doesn't deserve it." She turned and picked up the newspaper off the floor. In front of Dorothy, she flattened it smooth against the counter with her hands. She stood there a moment, looking down at it. At the top edge of her vision she could see Dorothy looking between her and Wilbur, from one to the other, like something had transpired between them, and she wanted to know what it was.

From out on the sidewalk, through the plate-glass window with *Millerville Gazette, Voice of a Valley* painted across it in bold letters, she saw Dorothy start in on her husband, her hand slam down on the counter, Belle's newspaper whisk off into the air, its pages separating and then settling onto the floor.

On down the sidewalk, out in the open air, Belle felt lighter and more hopeful than she had for some time. The sun was out and the clouds were oh-so-white against the blue sky. That was enough for her, at least for today.

LOG ENTRY: 8 November, 1939. The floor of the main span is finished, the grid welded, and the concrete poured. None of the floor extends to the side girders but is carried entirely on the stringers. The concrete was struck off even with the top of the steel I-beams, except along each side—there, an 8-inch curb was raised and a 4-inch reinforced concrete sidewalk was cantilevered over to approximately the center of the girders but was kept clear of the top of the girders. The curb and sidewalk were poured monolithically. Drains were provided through the floor every 50 feet. This light type floor was adopted to keep the dead load small and therefore the stress in the cables at a low figure.

CHAPTER 39

THE CROW

Buck Shyrock could look at the bridge now. It still made him sad, its being there, blocking a piece of the sky and marring his view of the river before it disappeared around the bend. But it was like August had said: you can't stop progress, the moving forward. It was life. The river proved that. The Wabash never stopped moving and changing.

Still, though, it wasn't the same thing. The bridge, to Buck's mind, erased a part of the river in the very act of connecting the two states, those separate pieces of land that were *meant* to be separate. The river never erased anything. The river was linked to all things and, because of that, joined together all as it was meant to be.

The railings were being fixed into place. He saw the welder's flash, smelled the burnt sulfur stink wafting past him in invisible clouds as he crossed on the ferry. This, he reckoned, was one of the final steps. It was almost complete.

Although he'd never get used to its being there and would always see it as a travesty to the river, he had to admit there was something oddly beautiful about the structure itself. It appeared almost to hover between the two banks, without obvious means of support, as unlikely in its presence as a thin spider web dangling between branches. It was hard to believe it could hold its own weight, much less carry a load of traffic.

With his life as a ferryman winding down, Shyrock still had no idea what he would do with himself. His queries about other work had left him empty-handed. When he asked around, inquired after jobs that he knew were open, all he got in return was a bemused smile and a polite "keep you in mind." But he never heard any more about it. He didn't really care to do anything else anyway. Ferrying was all he had ever wanted to do, and after so many years, it wouldn't be easy to switch to something else. The thought of being idle, though, scared the hell out of him. McNutt had told him he could remain in the house, rent-free, as long as he cared to, so there was that. Shyrock appreciated his kindness, but he also knew no one besides him would want to live in the antiquated house, and modernizing it would cost his employer more than the house was worth.

"Goin' to the big shebang, Shyrock?"

Buck snapped out of his daydream and looked at Eugene Frank, standing there at the ferry railing, also gazing at the bridge, as they made their way across the river. Eugene had a thick mustache and a lantern jaw that jutted forward like a battering ram every time he bit down on his chaw. He worked at the Standard Oil station, kitty-corner from the Ford garage.

"Nah, don't reckon I will."

"Why not? They're expectin' the biggest crowd ever ta come ta this town. I don't see how you could miss it."

"Nah, it's their doin', not mine."

"But don't ya wanna see a gov'nor? Two gov'nors, Illinois and Indianner both. Gonna be here at the same time. Can you believe it?" Eugene shook his head in awe. "I never even seen one gov'nor. S'posed ta be lotsa bigwigs. Millerville's gonna be in the spotlight, that's for sure."

"Gotta work, ya know," Buck responded. "The bridge won't be open for bus'ness, what with all the people standin' on it. Might be someone needin' to cross the river."

Buck checked the throttle level to see if there was any more juice left, but he had it going full-out. Sometimes people just liked to hear themselves talk. No harm in that, he reckoned, but why so many questions? *If Eugene wants ta talk so bad, he oughta do it with someone who's int'rested, and leave me out of it,* Shyrock thought. Then he laughed at himself. Had he always been such a contrary ass? He reckoned he had. The hell of it was, he'd probably miss the talk once everything had taken place.

"Here ya go," Shyrock said once the ferry had touched onto the Indiana bank. As Eugene drove his car off the deck of the ferry, Buck waved from his station at the bow. "Enjoy your cer'mony there, Eugene," he called. Suddenly, he was brimming with good will toward this man with whom, up until now, he'd only exchanged greetings at the filling station. It was always the same: he grabbed a can of oil off the rack between the two pumps and put it on McNutt's tab so there was no need even to go inside. Howdy-doo and thankee and that was that—back to the river he went. Strange, not thinking much about any of it. Just doing it, day after blessed day.

Buck stepped off the apron onto the sand, leaving the old motor chortling behind him. He leaned into the gradual incline of the bank, his right hand pressed into his thigh as he made his way up. When he reached the trees, he turned to look at the new bridge—and at the new Millerville.

The plain backs of the buildings on Main Street were aflame from the sun beginning to rise behind him, giving them a kind of special effervescence that they lacked in the shabby, everyday course of things. In this light, his simple house, painted an orangish-yellowish brown, looked like a palace on its promontory overlooking the great river. The bridge, although still only bare steel, shone in the soft light, arching gracefully over the river like a miracle that had materialized that very instant out of thin air, the way a rainbow suddenly appears. Yes, it would be a big shebang, no doubt about it, and the town would be proud. Who could blame them? They *should* be proud. It was about time some attention came their way. It wasn't such a bad place, and they weren't such a bad bunch when you took the time to think about it. Look how long they'd supported his and his family's ferry.

Buck turned and looked downriver where the current slowed to a crawl near the sandbar but pressed hard and fast over against the high Illinois bank, rising straight up to where the line of trees stood like an advancing army, halted by an impassible barrier. He cocked his ear, listening for the watery voice. If there was a time to hear it, this should be it, while everything was so soft and magical, like in a dream. But all he heard was the low gurgling of the boat motor and, echoing somewhere behind him, the *caw-caw* of a crow on the wing. Beyond the levee it flew, out over the flat bottomland, pursuing whatever designs crows pursued. The thing about a crow was they never quit. *You never see a crow lying on the ground, dying slowly,* he thought. *They keep going right up until the very end.* He'd seen one once, winging it across the river, easy as you please. Suddenly, it faltered and then fell straight from the sky into the river with a splash. The way it fell—it wings half-extended, stilled in mid-beat—he could tell it was dead before it hit the water.

So, back he would go, across to the town, where he would keep doing what he'd been doing for so long, until someone came and told him it was over—that there weren't any more folks needing to be ferried. From there, he would put one foot out in front of him, at least, and see if the other followed.

CHAPTER 40

THE RIVER'S A WOMAN

Holly loved Thanksgiving above all other days. It was when you were supposed to stop doing everything you usually did and just think about all the things you were lucky enough to have. Giving thanks—that's what everybody was supposed to do. No pretending, the way you did on Christmas, like you were excited about a present when really it was the very thing you'd hoped you wouldn't get.

She knew people called her a dreamer. "There she goes again," her dad would sometimes say. "Off in dreamland." And she knew that most of the other kids thought she was weird, the way she sat off by herself on the playground sometimes, looking at the shadows of leaves dancing on the side of the schoolhouse, or watching the clouds pass like gallant ships overhead. But she didn't care. Being a dreamer was a fine thing, to her mind.

Her gramps was a dreamer, his head all the time turned slightly sideways, listening, or looking off into the distance, even if he was inside his house. "You and me are tarred with the same brush," he'd told her that time he'd gotten her a drink of water. "Our minds are always somewheres else, 'stead of where other people think they should be." That had helped her a lot, him saying that. Her Gramps was a smart man. There was a lot going on behind those eyes of his, she could tell.

Maybe dreaming was just another way of giving thanks—paying special attention to what God has given to us, to his creation. A way of praying, sort of.

Walking to town to get flour for her mother, Holly felt excited; butterflies fluttered all around in her stomach. Tomorrow would be the day, her favorite day of the year.

Main Street was alive with cars coming and going, people calling to one another from across the street, laughing at some joke or other. Everyone was in a festive mood. "You have a nice Thanksgivin'," she heard more than once as she made her way on the sidewalk, concentrating hard on not skipping (which is what she wanted to do) now that she was more grown up. She knew every single soul that she saw. There was Irene Hanes, and there, getting into his car, was Charley Graves. Like always, across the street at the barbershop was Max Howard behind his big window, cigarette hanging from his mouth, comb and scissors in his hand. Today, he was giving that balding Harmon Rowe a holiday trim. Holly was in Max's barber shop with her dad once. After Harmon left, her dad said to Max, "You oughta feel bad, chargin' Harmon for a haircut when he ain't got any hair."

"I charge him for lookin' for it," Max answered. Her dad and Max had a good laugh over that one.

Holly loved saying people's names in her head. She used their full names without the Mister or Missus that she was taught to use when addressing them. It gave her a feeling of owning them. Not like they were property. She knew they were people and you couldn't own a person. It was hard to explain. Millerville was her town, and since they were part of Millerville, that made them her people, didn't it? She didn't really own them, yet they were hers just the same. That's how she felt anyway.

The grade school principal, Mr. Crowley (she didn't know his first name), stopped her on the sidewalk. "Hello, Holly. You certainly look spry today. Helping your mother get ready for tomorrow, are you?"

"Yes, sir. She sent me to get her some flour." Like most kids, she was a little afraid of Mr. Crowley. At school, he was always so strict-looking, peering at them through his round spectacles. He was tall, towering over all the kids, and every day he wore a gray suit and tie. But today he didn't look like a principal at all. He had on an open-collar shirt and baggy slacks. He looked happy, his usual scowl gone.

"Well, good for you," he said. "Helping your mother. I'm sure you're one of the things she'll be giving thanks for tomorrow."

"Thank you, Mr. Crowley," she responded, her neck craned upward. She smiled at him, and they went their separate ways.

Holly no longer felt threatened by Dan Abel, the grocer. Now, she found him funny—the way he almost ran everywhere, his nervous, deer-like face. Nowadays she said hello to him, smiled, and went on her way. That's how it was today. "Hello, Holly," he said in return, eyeing her cautiously.

On she went to the aisle where the baking goods were shelved. She stopped briefly at the cereal section where she had had her "brain spell." She stood waiting, holding her breath, to see if anything would happen, but there was nothing. She found it reassuring.

She grabbed the sack of flour, carried it to the front counter, and handed the money her mother had given her to the cashier.

"Hello, Miss Shyrock." It was Mary Hawthorne. She sat on a stool at the cash register all day because she couldn't walk or stand very well. Her cane hung from the counter next to her. She was Mr. Abel's wife's mother. According to Holly's mother, the grocery store had been run by Mary Hawthorne and her husband before he died. "Your mother must be makin' a pie for Thanksgivin'. Yum, yum, lucky girl," she exclaimed, rubbing her round tummy. "How ya doin' t'day?" she asked.

"Fine," Holly answered. And then she remembered her mother's admonition that it was rude to just give one-word answers and not ask after the other person. "I'm fine. And how are you, Mrs. Hawthorne?"

"Best I can expect, I reckon. You excited 'bout the new bridge gonna open? Ever'body seems to be plumb beside themselves with excitement."

"Yeah, I guess," Holly said.

"You guess! Sweetheart, this is big. *Real* big. I don't suppose you've been around long enough to know that."

"I guess not," Holly said.

"Well, maybe I'll see you at the cer'mony. Hard tellin' though. S'posed to be a whole stampede o' people gallopin' our way."

Holly gave her a weak smile. "Bye, Mrs. Hawthorne," she said and walked out the door.

Lugging her flour sack under one arm, Holly ducked into the narrow alley between buildings, taking a shortcut to where she was heading. There was all manner of stuff on the ground there, all of it worthless, she supposed, but she had once liked to pretend it was undiscovered treasure. While there were probably never any pirates on the Wabash, there must have been bandits in the olden days, back when her Gramps was a young man. Among the rubble were empty liquor bottles (some of them broken), filthy corks, and now and then a penny—even a dime once. There were musty paper bags and bills of sale, gotten wet and then dried so many times they were flattened into the ground, almost a part of it. She'd found a rusty hammer one time with the wooden handle broken off. She'd picked it up and given it to her Gramps.

"Maybe you can fix it," she'd said, handing it over.

He'd smiled big and said, "That'll make a mighty fine hammer, Lol. Look here. It's a *Barkley*!" He'd held the hammer in front of her and pointed at the name etched in the side. "The best hammer made. Nicer 'n the one I've got now. Thank you, sweetheart!"

Once she'd found an old photograph of a well-dressed lady, curled at the edges, a crease where it had been folded in half. It had been rained on. There was a big "X" scratched across the woman's face. Holly felt sorry for the woman, to have her fine picture end up this way. She took it home and put it with her drawings and her pictures of dresses she'd cut out of her mother's catalogs that someday, when she had her own money, she wanted to buy.

Now, everything she stepped on or over as she went along was old news to her. She hoped her Gramps was on this side of the river so she wouldn't have to wait for him. If she waited too long, her mother would want to know what kept her. She hated lying to her, hated it more than anything. It was best if she didn't take too long getting back home so she wouldn't have to answer any questions.

She knocked at his door, but there was no answer. There was only one place he could be, so she walked back across the yard and around to the top of the landing. There he was, sitting by the edge of the landing, his feet almost on the ferry's apron. He'd brought one of the kitchen chairs down to sit on.

Holly shouted to him and then headed on down the incline, being careful not to slip on the dirt and scattered rocks that littered the rough concrete surface. She was supposed to wait for him to come to her, but after watching her Gramps labor to the top of the landing, Holly only did that once. The second time, she did like today. He'd looked at her with that keen look of his and let it pass.

"Hi there, Gramps," she said cheerfully once she'd reached his side.

"Well, if it ain't my Lol!" he exclaimed. He reached around her waist, pulling her to him. "You're a sight for sore eyes, darlin'. Here, sit on my lap."

"I'm too big," she protested, even as she did what he asked.

"Not yet," he said, "but maybe soon."

Once settled, Holly looked out at the river. "Is it still not talking to you?"

He sighed. "Nope, but I keep waitin'. I was sittin' here thinkin' that maybe she's mad at me for somethin' I've done. And that's why she's givin' me the silent treatment."

"What could you have done that made her so mad?"

"I dunno. I reckon she ain't gonna tell me neither. Might never know."

Holly turned and looked in his eyes. "Gramps, why do you say 'her' when you talk about the river?"

"It just came to me once't." He reached up and brushed the hair back off her forehead. "I dunno why. It just came to me."

Holly kept quiet after that. They sat and watched the river together. The sun hid behind a cloud and then just as quickly burst out again, illuminating the river's surface in a flare of light. The bare trees over on the other bank stood motionless. In fact, besides the river effortlessly slipping past, the occasional fish breaking the surface and splashing down again, and the few clouds shifting in the sky, nothing moved. All was quiet up on the bridge; the building crew, now in the process of installing the railings, must have taken an afternoon break. From across the water came the sounds of work on the connecting road over in Indiana, far back around the levee that snaked off to the northeast along the low-lying woods bordering the river. Closer to them, Holly and her grandfather could hear the slurp of the current passing under the ferry, and the muffled pre-holiday hustle-bustle up on Main Street.

Shyrock began haltingly. "I figure the river is a woman," he said, "'cause men ain't able to stay mad. Not so long anyhow." He shook his head, trying to clear his thoughts and start over. "Nah, that ain't what I meant to say, though it's true enough. I reckon what I do mean is a man ain't able to go so deep as a woman. A river knows ever'thin' there is to know. Ever'thin', Lolli." He stopped again, arranging his thoughts. He scratched at his big ear. "A man might think he knows ever'thin', but he don't. And whatever he does know, he full well tells ya all about it. A woman, she keeps quiet 'bout what she knows until she's good and ready to say it. And she knows plenty, believe you me. She knows plenty. You'll see some day," he added, patting Holly on the arm. "You'll know more 'n your granddaddy ever dreamed o' knowin'.

"Once in a great while," he continued, "once in a very great while, the river lets go some o' her secrets. You'll see what I'm talkin' 'bout, Lol. You'll see, 'cause you know enough to wait. Maybe that's part o' the trouble—I ain't got the patience I used ta have."

Holly leaned back against his chest. She felt one of the buttons on his bib overalls pressing into her skin, but she didn't move. She liked the feel of his breath going in and out, entering his lungs and then leaving. She slowed down her own breathing so it was in rhythm with his. She thought she could go to sleep just listening to his rough voice and feeling his chest rise and fall against her back.

"Your grandma," he said, his voice only a whisper now, "your grandma used ta do that. She'd get all mad at me about somethin'—sometimes I knew what and sometimes I didn't—and she wouldn't say boo to me for a day or two. Just keep silent as a dust mote. I'd end up almost beggin' her to talk to me, it got to me so."

Holly felt a little jerk to his breathing, like maybe she was too heavy, leaning against his chest, so she sat up straight. "I guess she felt sorry for me, 'cause then she'd forgive me whatever it was I'd done, and we'd go on like nothin' had happened."

Holly turned to look at him, and she could see the wet behind his eyes. "Gramps, the river'll talk to you again, just like Grandma did. You wait and see."

He gently pressed her off his lap. "I don't know 'bout that, Lol. The river might not be as forgivin' as your grandma. We'll see, I reckon. You better be gettin' on home."

She hugged him tight around the neck and then tucked the flour sack under her arm. She ran up the landing, making up for lost time so her mother wouldn't ask too many questions. "See you tomorrow!" she yelled, and over the top she flew, her dark curls fanning out like unfurled wings.

≈ ≈ ≈

Holly burst into the kitchen with all the breathlessness and wide-eyed excitement of a young girl who's just been out in the world, even if in a small, measured way. Leaning into the table and opening her arms so the flour plopped onto its surface, she blurted, "Did you know the river's a woman?"

Immediately she realized her mistake, but it was too late. All she could do now was snap her traitorous lips shut and stand there looking like the proverbial cat with the canary hidden in its mouth.

"You've been talking to your grandfather," Belle said, turning away from the sink. She pummeled her hands against a red-and-white checked dishtowel, as if she was punishing them for getting wet.

Holly's facial expression didn't change, but her eyes darted around the room.

"Okay, out with it," Belle said. She folded her arms and leaned against the cabinet.

"Hmm?" Holly said.

"You saw your granddad. Where was he?"

Holly's face closed up, and she wouldn't say another word. She'd swallowed the canary, and no amount of talk was going to make it come out again.

God, she can be stubborn when she sets her mind to something, Belle thought. "Okay, go and wash your hands and come back and help me."

≈ ≈ ≈

"Do you know that our daughter is stopping by to see her grandfather on her way back from the store?" Belle asked. She lay on her side in their bed, facing August, her head propped up by her arm.

He lay on his back, looking at the ceiling. "Really?"

"Yes, really. I've suspected it for a while. She comes home with mosquito bites all over, twigs in her hair, smelling of the river, a dreamy look in her eye. Today after going to town, she says to me, 'Did you know the river's a woman?'" Belle covered her mouth, trying not to laugh. "You should have seen her face."

August raised his eyebrows. "Yep, she could only have gotten that from the old man. If you knew, why haven't you said something to her? And to Dad. We've told her to stay away from the river. It's dangerous. He should know that."

"Oh, I'm sure Dad keeps on eye on her. There's nothing that gets anywhere close to the ferry landing that he doesn't know about."

"But she's disobeying, and he's encouraging her. That's all there is to it."

"I'm fairly certain that seeing his granddaughter is good medicine for Dad. There's a connection there that I can't quite put my finger on. Two peas in a pod, those two. So I've decided to leave it alone, at least for now."

"Okay then," August said. "Suit yourself. But I don't like it. We'll see if he says anything."

"Oh, he won't. Not if I know Dad. Keepin' a secret with his granddaughter is like a blood oath to him. We couldn't drag it out of him no matter how hard we tried." Belle smiled, pinching the bed covers between her fingers. "The really silly thing about it is that he feels bad. I'm sure he does. Keeping it from us. But a secret is a secret. You men and your pride. Rather die than give up an ounce of it."

"I reckon that's all we got when you come right down to it."

"Oh, brother," Belle responded. "You poor thing." She kissed his fingertips, in spite of herself.

He took hold of her hand and kissed its smooth back. "Good thing I've got you," he said. "What a miserable wretch I'd be without you."

"But a *proud* wretch," she said. "A proud, miserable wretch." They both laughed, quietly, so as to not wake the girls.

Belle flopped over onto her back and joined him in staring at the ceiling. "What was it like," she asked, "after so much time has passed?"

Although it had been over a month, he knew she was talking about his piloting the ferry the day his dad's dog was killed.

"It's hard to say," August answered.

"What do you mean, 'hard to say'?"

"I don't know what to think, much less how to say it."

"It must've brought back memories."

"Yeah, that."

"Any pleasant memories? Something you'd like to share with your wife?" She turned back on her side and laid her hand on his chest.

"Not a memory, exactly. But it did hit me that it's really *over*. Back when I hated it, when I was forced to do it, it seemed like it would never end. All I could see was my life stretching out in front of me, crossing the river on that old rack of wood, back and forth without end. But now I can see it. That last trip'll be made, and it'll just end." He snapped his fingers. "Finished, just like that. I'm gonna miss it, that old ferry." He let go of a deep sigh. "The last ferryman."

"Can you imagine how your dad must feel then?"

"No. No, I can't."

They let the notion hover in the air above them, neither talking, but their thoughts somehow following the same path. Facts are not the real truths. The final rubbing against shore of the ferry's apron—that's not what's real, but the feelings. Their feelings, Holly's feelings, August's father's feelings—that's what's real. Such truths cannot be spoken, not with any degree of accuracy, not even in a quiet, moonlit bedroom at night.

Finally, it was Belle who broke the silence. "I wish you could have seen him that day, watching you. I don't know how to say this, but for him, that was the end. Watching you operate the ferry—his only surviving child, his son. It was like you memorialized it for him. He saw it. He saw its end, and it was beautiful to him because of you. It didn't even matter that you walked away from it before. Maybe for him, you're the last ferryman. And for him, the rest is just going through the motions." She leaned and kissed August on the mouth. "I'm proud of you," she whispered.

August tried to think of something to say to let Belle know he'd heard her, everything she had said. But he was afraid that after her heartfelt words, spoken in her melodic, lyrical voice, his would be like so much static on the radio, cluttering the room, scratching at the air, lacking substance.

He looked at her, luminescent among the shadows, gazing at him with her loving eyes. She was so beautiful, he had to reach out and touch her again to make sure she was real and not a mirage. Yes, without her he was indeed a miserable wretch. He was no stranger to emotion—he had lots of feelings, but mostly he lacked the words to give them voice. They just swam around in circles like fish trapped in a tank. He could often find the words for his girls, and sometimes with Belle, but never the way Belle could. She had the easy, fluid grace of a poet.

LOG ENTRY: 20 November, 1939. The handrails, consisting of wire mesh on steel angles, supported by 6-inch I-beam posts spaced about 8 feet on centers, have been fully installed. The original plans showed the wire mesh continuous over the entire length of the bridge. I suggested that the wire mesh be made up in panels rather than continuous, so any panel that became damaged could be replaced without affecting any other panel. This change was made. The handrail was designed so as not to obstruct the view any more than necessary and still protect the traffic.

CHAPTER 41

THE TOE HOUSE

It was just about the silliest-looking thing Buck had ever seen. It stood at the Indiana side of the bridge, in the middle of the two lanes, just before the highway became bridge deck. Because the trees had been cleared out to give the construction crew a wide swath, Buck could see it from the ferry landing, planted there in the road like an outhouse with windows. For the life of him, he couldn't figure out why they had put it there. After August had said the blessing, he asked about it.

"It's the toll booth," John Welch said, across the table from him. "It's how they'll pay for the bridge, by taking tolls from them who use it." Belle had invited Welch to the holiday meal when she'd had a chance meeting with him at the post office. Blushing because, stupidly, she had never thought about it until that moment, that he might have nowhere to go on Thanksgiving, she insisted that he come. "Be at Dad's by noon," she'd said, walking away before he had time to refuse.

"Toll *what*?" Buck said, still not getting why the odd-looking structure was there.

"A toll *booth*, Dad," Belle said, taking her seat at the table next to Vivian, who was perched on an empty, upside-down bolt box set atop her chair. The girl glanced around the table at everyone, smiling happily, amazed at her new grown-up perspective on the world.

"A toe boot," Vivian said loudly, wanting to make sure others noticed her. "It sounded wike Mista Wewch said 'toe boot.' Wike a witto bitty boot for a toe," Vivian squealed, squirming atop her little throne, cracked up by her own joke.

"Careful," Belle said, steadying her with her hand.

"Hawwy, what do you caw a *boat* for a toe?" Vivian asked, just getting warmed up.

Holly rolled her eyes. "A toe boat," she said. "That's just dumb."

"It is too funny," Welch said. "Vivian, whattaya call a rope tied around a toe?"

"A toe wope!" Vivian screeched.

Belle held her finger to her lips. "Shh, too loud," she said.

"Well then, whattaya call a house where toes live?" Welch again.

"A toe house!"

"Righto!" Welch exclaimed, and then, "Sorry, Belle." He covered his smile. "I'll stop now."

August steered the conversation away from the various accoutrements for toes, back to the topic at hand. "Dad, you know, a toll is like someone paying to cross the ferry. Except you always called it a fare. It's the same thing."

"What if they don't stop?" Holly asked, looking at her dad.

The adults all laughed, except for Buck. Joining in the merriment, Vivian kicked at the bottom of the table, trying to shift the attention back to her. "A toe house!" she squealed. Belle put her hand on the girl's leg and gave her a stern look.

Buck, sitting next to Holly, looked down at her and winked his approval. "By my way o' seein' it," he said, "that's a darn sensible question. On the ferry, see, it don't leave the landing 'til everyone's paid." Then he added, "Or until arrangements are made for later payment."

"Or unless you take it outta your own pocket," John Welch said. "I saw that more 'n once."

Buck shrugged his shoulders, as if to say, *What're you gonna do?* He passed the milk gravy to Holly as he asked Welch, "So you mean a fella's meant to sit in it then?"

"Yep, and collect the toll," Welch said.

"Seems awful small for that. I mean, for a fella to sit in all day."

"Well, Dad, that's how it's done nowadays," said August. "They got 'em all over. There's some up by Chicago for the highways. Same thing. They collect a toll until the cost of building the road's paid off."

"Hmmm," Buck said, still not wholly convinced.

"I got an idea, Gramps," Holly said. "You can carry those on the ferry who don't want to pay to cross the bridge."

"They'd still have to pay, sweetheart," Belle explained.

"I betcha Gramps'd do it for free, wouldn'tcha, Gramps?"

Buck laid his hand on top of Holly's bushy hair as she looked up at him admiringly. "I reckon, given half a chance, I would, Lol. Yep, reckon I would at that."

"Yeah!" Vivian shouted, striking the butt of her knife on the table. "And I would help. Fer nothin'."

"Okay, girls, enough talk. You need to eat. Your mom worked hard at this meal," August said.

Buck caught each of the girls' eyes and made the sign: *Zip your lip*. Vivian pursed hers and wrinkled her nose at him, but she kept quiet.

"Thank ya's" and "by gollys" and "mighty goods" directed at Belle traveled around the table. When the turkey platter came to Vivian, she stubbornly insisted on helping herself. Belle held the platter while she forked a piece of turkey, dropping it twice on the tablecloth before it landed on her plate. "Zip yo' wip, mista tuhkey," she said.

CHAPTER 42

THE PROPOSAL

John Welch had known the plan before sitting down at the Thanksgiving table, but he still hadn't found the opportune time to discuss it with Shyrock. In the drugstore for coffee one day, Sal had informed him that Floyd Bailey wanted to speak with him. "Something important" was all she knew. Welch told Sal to let Floyd know he'd be there for breakfast two days from then.

Floyd Bailey seemed shy at first. He had finished his breakfast before Welch arrived, and his ticket and money lay on the counter. When Welch plopped down on the stool next to him, Floyd's handshake was lackluster, absent its usual vigor. "Morning, John," he said.

"Good mornin' to ya, Floyd."

Sal made it her business to stay out of the way of a serious conversation about to take place. From behind the counter, she caught Welch's eye while standing a few steps away from the two men. "Just coffee, Sal. Thank you."

It had always surprised Welch the way a warm, rousing friendship could cool in so short a time, from simple, often unintentional neglect. Even though this time it was agreed upon, their paths, it seemed, had gone in nearly opposite directions—Floyd's in erecting the future, Welch's in trying to patch together remnants of the past. It was almost as if they had nothing to talk about.

Floyd wasted no time. "I'll get to the point," he said, fingering his nearly empty coffee cup. "I've done some checking, called in some favors. What I'm trying to say is, the toll booth job is open."

Welch looked at him, puzzled.

"In some ways, it'll be perfect," Floyd continued. "The ferry ends; the bridge begins. The walk will be a little further." Floyd attempted a smile, but it fell short in a sad, sheepish sort of way.

"What are you sayin', Floyd?"

"The toll booth is Mr. Shyrock's, if he wants it."

"The toll booth."

"Yes, the job is his."

It was such a far-fetched idea, so wildly humorous—the picture of Shyrock squatting on a stool, crowded into a toll booth like a coon in a hollow tree trunk—that Welch couldn't stifle a laugh. "Do you mean to say, Shyrock, collecting tolls?"

Floyd Bailey looked a little hurt, but Welch could see that he had expected this reaction. That's likely why he was acting so discomfited this morning, Welch realized.

"I know it's hard to imagine, but think about it," Floyd persisted. "He's not ready to stop working. It won't require any physical strain, it's close to home, and most important, he'll still be on the river."

Welch couldn't help but be impressed, as well as moved. Floyd had given this some thought. With all the other things on his plate, he had remembered Shyrock's predicament. Sure, it was a stretch, but he himself hadn't come up with anything better. "I'm sorry I laughed, Floyd. You're very kind."

"No, no, I get it. I thought the same thing myself, at first. But there's some sense in it, the more you ponder it."

The early sun, just showing itself over the tops of the trees across the river, had wormed itself between buildings and now reflected off the plate-glass windows opposite the drugstore. Suddenly, the interior of the store was bathed in an orange glow. Seated beside him at the counter, Welch witnessed Floyd's face opening up—every minute pore, every wrinkle squiggling away from his squinted eyes, and every missed whisker on his freshly shaved face revealed. At that moment, John Welch saw him, really *saw* him, for the first time. Never had he known a more guileless and selfless man than Floyd Bailey. There was absolutely nothing in his proposal for himself. Regardless of its improbability, no matter how harebrained it may seem, Welch believed so much in the goodness of that face that he decided to move ahead on Floyd's idea.

"Well, Floyd, I reckon there's only one way to find out. By askin' the man hisself," he said.

Welch tried to implant the memory of Floyd's smile in his brain so its light would still shine in him when he carried his message forward to Shyrock.

CHAPTER 43

STUFFED BUT STILL STANDING

The overpowering paint smell took the fresh air hostage. More than once while crossing the river, an especially thick cloud of the noxious stuff crossed paths with the ferry, so that Buck and whatever passengers he carried were forced to cover their faces with their coat sleeves. It took two weeks to the day to layer the entire bridge with two coats of paint. By the time it was done, Buck's coat and the ferry were speckled with tiny green dots.

It wasn't a green that Shyrock cared for. It was akin to what he'd seen once in one of the baby's diapers.

Now that the bridge was nearing completion, the tone of his relations with his passengers, always muted and sparse before, had taken on a different timbre. Paying little attention to the now-familiar bridge, they looked at him in a longing way, like he was going away, never to be seen again. They wanted to reminisce about the "old days." They treated Buck like a hero and a legend, and it riled him to no end. If he deserved any medals, it was for putting up with them during these final days.

"I sure have missed that old dog o' your'n," said one old-timer, Lester Ballard, who was in bad need of a shave and a face washing. "Ever' boat needs a mascot, I reckon." He stood on deck in front of the steer boat, nearly blocking

Shyrock's line of sight. His Model T pickup—rusted in more spots than not, its cloth top ripped and tattered, its rear springs completely shot—sat with its back end low to the deck. Lester leaned over the rail and blew snot out of one nostril. Buck looked away. After wiping his hand on a filthy pant leg, Lester gave Shyrock a slanted look and said, "A dog wards off the bad luck, they say."

He waited for Buck to respond, and when he didn't, Lester said, "Whatcha reckon they gonna do with the ol' ferry?"

Shyrock shrugged his shoulders. "I reckon no one's thought o' that." He himself hadn't until now. He hated to think of the ferry rotting away behind some barn somewhere, raided for scrap, a haven for woodchucks and rats and damp-seeking snakes. "Don't matter much," he said.

"A museum, mebbe," Old Man Ballard said. "None close around, though."

Buck laughed. "A museum. That's a good one, Lester. They could stuff me and stand me up right here in the steer boat."

Lester Ballard laughed, too, but he watched Shyrock out of the corner of his eye. He'd heard it said that Shyrock had one oar out of the water since this whole bridge business had commenced.

LOG ENTRY: 5 December, 1939. The steel superstructure was given two coats of paint; primarily, of course, to protect the steel, but the green shade was chosen as better to blend the slender towers and the graceful lines of the cables and stiffening girders with the natural beauty of the surrounding countryside. The resulting bridge is not only of definite value to the community but also a monument to its foresight and enterprise.

In this connection, it might do well to mention that the citizens of Millerville took a great interest in the construction of this bridge. So-called "sidewalk superintendents" were first recognized when observation windows were installed for spectators during the erection of buildings in Rockefeller Center in New York City. While no efforts were made for their comfort at this bridge, visitors were welcome as long as they kept clear of the work. The attached picture shows 18 "sidewalk superintendents" on the job.

Construction of this bridge began in January of this year, and despite much high water during its early months, it will be ready for traffic as soon as the paint dries and the dedication has taken place.

To me, it was a privilege and a pleasure to have been chosen as project engineer for this job and to have had a part in the building of a bridge of such a unique design.

CHAPTER 44

THE OFFER

Grabbing a few moments to speak privately with Shyrock, without interruption, was a tricky and sensitive proposition. Welch knew once he started, he had to finish or, in all likelihood, he wouldn't get another go at it. Shyrock would shut him out like some pesky Jehovah's Witness, and that would be the end of it. The mere hint of Floyd Bailey's offer after that would be like offering Shyrock a dose of poison. Welch couldn't think of a better time than dinnertime.

In Millerville, at straight-up noon, the fire whistle sent its wailing howl out across the town and surrounding countryside. You could almost hear the clank of lunch pails opening in unison. The drugstore filled up, and farmers headed for their houses. As a result, the riverbanks were devoid of human activity. Shyrock would be at his house, piecing together a meal, and after that, catching a few nods. Disturbing his nap wouldn't get Welch started off on the right foot. It was now or never.

When Welch arrived, Buck was leaning over his meager meal, saying grace. His big fists were folded together over the table, his bowed forehead pressed against them. Welch waited for him to finish before he rapped at the door.

"Yep!" Shyrock yelled. "It's open!" When Welch was in, Buck said, "I'd offer ya somethin', but this is about it."

"It's all right. I already had a bite to eat," Welch lied. He was so nervous about talking with Buck, he'd had no appetite for food.

"Glass o' water?"

"Sure."

"Help yourself, if ya don't mind."

Stalling, Welch took his time. He looked out the window over the hand pump and studied the clouds that had turned all gauzy, as if the whole sky was a festering wound. He took notice of the crummy store-backs, somber in the dreary daylight. He topped off the glass with a last coax of the pump handle and returned to the table.

Seeing Shyrock labor at his meal, chewing at a dry piece of beef like he expected it to bring him no sustenance or pleasure, Welch felt defeated before he'd even begun. He pictured Floyd Bailey's bright smile at the drugstore and then just plowed into it, head first. "You remember tellin' me you wouldn't know what to do with yourself once the ferry ended?"

"Nope, don't remember it," Shyrock said, seeing the seriousness on Welch's face, thinking of the business-like sound of his first step onto the porch, and all the times he was trying to do his job, and Welch giving him grief.

Welch hesitated, too focused on his task to see that Shyrock was toying with him. "Well," he said, flustered, "it's like this." Knowing of Shyrock's hard feelings toward Floyd Bailey since that first day on the riverbank, he was careful not to mention his name. "I was talkin' to this fella at the drugstore 'bout a job."

"John Welch, a druggist? Who'd a thunk it?" Shyrock said, not looking up from his plate. "I always figgered ya needed some type o' special schoolin' fer a job like that."

"Goddamn it all, Shyrock, would you shut up and listen!"

"Okay, okay. Don't git yer dander up. Is this the bridge feller then?"

Welch felt his jaw drop.

"I know ya been talkin' to him from the beginnin'. Criminently, Welch, you oughta know. Ya can't scrape shit off yer boots in this town without everyone knowin' 'bout it."

"Floyd Bailey," Welch said, still stunned.

"A man can talk to who he wants," Buck said, grabbing his water glass. "C'mon, Welch, out with whatever ya come to tell me about."

"He said—Floyd Bailey, that is—said you can have the toll booth job if you want it." Welch blurted it out. It wasn't at all the way he'd rehearsed, laying out the logic of Floyd's idea: right timing as far as the ferry ending, close to his house, close to the river, easy to do for a man getting on in years.

Shyrock looked at him now, his eyes scrunched up as he studied Welch's face. He'd been about to fork into some kernel corn, but instead he laid the fork next to his plate, taking care that it was lined up straight. "The hell you say," he said, finally.

"That's what he said."

"How much is he payin'?"

"The job is workin' for the Indiana highway, I reckon, not him."

"How much?" Shyrock was looking at him shrewdly, his mouth screwed up as if numbers were tumbling through his brain.

Welch didn't like the look. It was something he'd never seen before on his friend's face. "Don't know. You'll have to ask someone else that question."

"Don't *he* know?"

"Never knew you to care about money, Shyrock."

"It's time I do."

"Okee-doke," Welch said. "I can at least ask him."

Welch was flabbergasted. He had expected Shyrock to flat-out tell him to leave. Not only that, Shyrock had changed, in no time at all, from the humble man of prayer to the shrewd potential wage-earner. He wished he could say he liked the upshot of his visit.

"That it? What ya come for?" said Shyrock.

"I reckon it is."

Shyrock pushed himself away from the table, the old chair creaking and popping under him. "Well, then. It's time for my two winks."

Outside, Welch hoisted one foot up onto the running board of his pickup and hauled himself in behind the wheel, thinking, *Ain't life strange? And the people in it.*

$$\approx \approx \approx$$

It didn't take long for Buck to decide. He couldn't let his granddaughters watch him give up, and if he sat around the house with nothing to do, that's exactly what would happen. He was as sure of it as he'd ever been of anything. Holly and Vivian would see him shrivel up like an old prune, and that would be their memory of him—a broken-down old man.

What did he think about being the toll taker? He wasn't a fool. His body was slowly wearing out, and this was something he could do. And he would be by the river. Not *on* it, like he always had been, but at least *over* it. Shyrock had pretty much given up on the river ever talking to him again anyway, so it wouldn't matter so much, him being, in all likelihood, out of earshot. As long he could see it and smell it and feel its presence, he would get by. This he told himself, willing himself to believe it.

It was the best he could expect.

He had taken to peering over there in the evenings from his porch. August said it was called a "toll booth," but the "toe house" is how he now thought of it, remembering Thanksgiving and the little jokester, Vivian, with a smile. He tried picturing himself behind the glass windows of the toe house, stuffed in there all day like a banana in its peel, but no matter how many times he tried, he couldn't conjure it up. He would just have to get used to it. Like anything else, it would become a habit.

He'd learned that the hard way, more than once—Ida, baby Elizabeth, August leavin', Rebel the hound, and now the ferry. Doin' without. Movin' through to the next thing without stoppin' to consider if it fit with your new self or not. He could do it again.

This, too, he willed himself to believe.

He didn't care about the money, even though he let on to Welch that he did. He had a nose like a hound, that one. As usual, Shyrock didn't feel like explaining himself to anyone. Some of what he'd been thinking couldn't be explained, even to himself.

Shyrock rolled from his bed, grunting like an old mule, and headed for his boots. No two winks today.

CHAPTER 45

ALWAYS AND AGAIN

It was a cool day, the air brisk against Shyrock's face, but the sun shone like it thought it was summer. The bridge with its new coats of paint, dry now but still emitting a strong odor that tingled in his nostrils, gleamed in the bright daylight. Its red, white, and blue bunting, draped on the towers and all along both rails, gave it a whimsical look, as if it would be dismantled, a mere toy, after today's festivities were over and the crowd gone home.

Buck had never seen so many people in one place. He had been busy all morning, carting them and their vehicles back and forth across the river. The bridge was covered with people, shouting and pointing and moving about, peering over the sides. Parents grabbed their children's hands if they got too close to the rail, and all of those assembled set a gauge on the bridge and its new presence in their lives. The crowd spilled well over both ends of the bridge—those not on it wanting to be. With the ribbon-cutting ceremony about to commence, everyone who was coming seemed to have arrived.

After tying off the ferry, Buck had dragged a wooden chair from the house and set it at the end of the landing by the water. The river had quickened over the course of the morning, cantering like a young filly. It intended to be noticed by the gathered throng, Shyrock believed, not to be outdone by the flash and flair of a new bridge. *It* was the reason for the bridge in the first place. *It* had to be accommodated. *It* hadn't changed, not one iota. The Wabash—the mighty Wabash.

Buck heard Vivian first. From the top of the landing she screamed, "I want to go *now*!" He turned in his chair, and there was his family, just starting down the ramp: Belle and Holly holding hands; Vivian leaning away from August, who pulled her along.

"Lookee here!" Buck shouted, waving them down to him.

Halfway down, Belle called out to him. "Come with us, Dad. We'll go together."

"Yeah, Gramps!" Holly said excitedly. "Come on!"

Once they were at his side, Buck said, "Look at y'all, decked out all fancy and nice." On August's and Belle's faces, all the worry and concern he had caused was plain as day.

Still pulling at August's hand, Vivian pointed at the bridge. "Theah! I wanna go *theah*!"

Buck laughed. "Hold on, little stick. You're gonna get there soon enough." Vivian gave him a quick, piercing look and then shouted, "Let's go! Let's *go*!" She yanked at her father's hand.

"Y'all go on," Buck said. "I'll watch it from here. Best seat in the house, the way I figure."

"I'll stay with Gramps," Holly said, looking up at her mother.

"Nah, sweetheart, you go." Shyrock looked over at the bridge and pointed. "That's your future right there. You oughta be up close, hearin' ever'thin' that's bein' said. Someday you can say, 'I was there.'"

Belle gave him an appraising look, but in front of the girls, she let it pass.

As the others started up the ramp, Buck waved August back. "Maybe you oughtn't go clear out on the deck with those girls. It don't look safe. Too many people for its bit o' strength."

August chuckled, laying his hand on his father's shoulder. He gave him a long look. "We'll see, Dad," he said.

At the top of the landing, still holding her mother's hand, Holly gazed back at Shyrock, a sad look on her face, like she wasn't so sure anymore whether what she thought the river had told her was right. But he winked at her and pointed her forward.

From his chair, Buck heard the voice on the loudspeakers start up. "Testing. Testing. One, two, three. Elizabeth, Mary, and Joseph. Testing." A titter of laughter went through the crowd. "Turn it up a wee bit," the tinny amplified voice said. Its echo bounced from bank to bank, on down the river, and Shyrock had the urge to turn, as if he could watch it go.

Then came a different voice, saying, "Please clear a path for our esteemed dignitaries. Clear a path. There you go." The man cleared his throat. "Move back some to give them room here at the podium. Thank you. . . . Okay, now, move back. More. Some more yet. Go on now. We need to get started. Thank you." Shyrock could see where the crowd parted, compressed even more on the Indiana side near the "toe house," the name again bringing a smile to his lips.

Next, he heard the Millerville Grade School seventh- and eighth-grade choir introduced. They sang "On the Banks of the Wabash, Far Away" and "Illinois," the crowd applauding at the end of each song. Only the singers closest to the single microphone could be heard; all the rest were consigned to the general murmur of the crowd. There were other songs by other groups. After the music was over, so-and-so and so-and-so and what's-his-chops (Buck's mother's old phrase for it) were introduced, all muckety-mucks, Buck reckoned. The crowd clapped after each speech. The Illinois governor's representative—*the honorable governor sends his regrets that he couldn't attend this historic occasion honoring the vision and fortitude of the Wabash Valley's great citizens*—said a few words, his voice alternately carried by a pocket of air to Shyrock's ears, clear as a bell, and then suddenly sounding all smothered, as if a gunny sack had been thrown over it. *Honorable, my eye,* thought Shyrock. *Not enough votes in this part of the state to make it worth his while.*

He hoped that his family, especially the girls, were close enough to hear what was being said but not on the bridge itself. No, that'd be too close. He wondered where John Welch was in all this. Probably as close to the action as he could weasel himself. He was one for the making of history, that Welch.

And then the Indiana governor took the podium. Shyrock could tell from the start that he would be long-winded. From the sound of his voice, you'd have thought he built the bridge himself, single-handedly. *"I am important,"* his tone seemed to say. *"Therefore I will take all the time I want."*

Shyrock shifted in his chair and waited for the governor to pick up a head of steam. Most people who liked to hear themselves speak, he'd observed, eventually did pick up a head of steam, their talk getting all lofty—more about them, typically, than the job at hand. When they did, there was no stopping them.

The historic speech came to him in jerks and starts. The main players were named. Something about a Robinson and a Steinman. The governor was naming the bridges that were designed by them all across the country. Vincennes Steel Corporation was mentioned. Wisconsin Bridge and Iron Company. Where other bridges like this one were built. He heard Pittsburgh, Pennsylvania. He heard Pan American Highway in Guatemala. The design was used "extensively" in Europe but none quite like this one. Self-supporting. No, none as special as this one. He heard when it was commenced. The exact hour of its finishing. On and on.

He only half-listened, and then he stopped listening at all. His eyes and his ears were on the river. For them, it was all about the bridge. For him, it was the river. Always, and again, the river.

A great, unified shout woke him out of his reverie. The ribbon had been cut.

Later on, when no one was around, he would go up and have a look for himself. See what it was about. Stick his toe in the "toe house."

ACKNOWLEDGMENTS

I would like to thank Loma Huh for helping me make numerous editorial improvements to this book. It is better because of her efforts.

Thanks to Mary Jo Rains for her generosity in giving me her scrapbook filled with photographs and old newspaper clippings pertaining to the Hutsonville ferry and the bridge that replaced it.

Thanks to Chuck Derry, Mike Sharp, Rose Thelen, Lee LaDue, Dean Severson, Midge and David Nusbaum, Chas and Jan Randle, and Tom and Liz Gannon for their enthusiasm, encouragement, and support.

I would also like to acknowledge and thank the Library of Congress for the use of its invaluable resources, both pictures and data files, available on its website.

Finally, my gratitude goes out to Allison, Kate, and Marna and all of the people at Langdon Street Press, whose editorial, creative, and technical expertise brought this book to fruition.

ABOUT THE AUTHOR

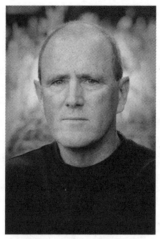

Photo by Adam Sparks

GREGORY RANDLE grew up on the Wabash River in southeastern Illinois. He was raised to have a wary respect for the river, hearing stories of its bounty as well as its hidden dangers. Later, when he was old enough to patch holes in an old wooden boat and operate a small motor loaned to him by his grandfather, Randle spent hours on the river reveling in its wildness and beauty. He now lives in Minnesota with his wife and two sons. This is his first novel.